AF491602

My Boss

Van Cole

Published by Van Cole, 2023.

This is a work of fiction. Similarities to real people, places, or events are entirely coincidental.

MY BOSS

First edition. June 13, 2023.

Copyright © 2023 Van Cole.

ISBN: 979-8223397410

Written by Van Cole.

Table of Contents

© Copyright 2021 by Van Cole All rights reserved.

In no way is it legal to reproduce, duplicate, or transmit any part of this document in either electronic means or in printed format. Recording of this publication is strictly prohibited and any storage of this document is not allowed unless with written permission from the publisher. All rights reserved.

Respective authors own all copyrights not held by the publisher.

My Boss
Gay First Time Enemies To Lovers Romance

By: Van Cole

Foreword

I would never have imagined meeting Stuart Glendon. But now he's my boss.

I applied for the job to work as the personal assistant to the actor I've crushed on since I was fifteen. And I got it. Now, I am so very confused. He is the most sexy, gorgeous man I have ever seen, but unfortunately the press says he's straight. Or at least, if he isn't, they have never mentioned – in fact, they mention quite the opposite, quite often. Somehow, though, I get the feeling that he likes me. Or he hates me – I don't know which anymore. We're so different. But, whatever the case is, we're both stuck in this tiny town until the film is shot. And it seems like something wonderful is about to happen.

My Boss

Chapter 1: Bennet

I looked up as someone walked across the bare floorboards. The house – when it was normally occupied – must have been quite cozy. But now, with the film crew having moved in two days before, it was bare and the sounds echoed. I felt my own heart thumping. Who was coming? I was in Oldham – a tiny town of perhaps a few hundred people – and the only inhabitants I'd seen so far had been people here to shoot the movie "Hot Shot"; a Western set in a small, prosperous town. I looked up as someone walked in and found myself looking at the producer, Mr. Lawford.

"Good morning, sir," I said. I'd met him yesterday, so that's how I knew who he was. He was about the same age as my dad, with gray hair, a smart suit and a worried expression. He nodded to me.

"You're Bennet Halton?" He asked me. He hadn't remembered, clearly, which I might have been put out about, except that I was far too excited to care. I was here! On the film set of a film that starred Stuart Glendon.

Stuart Glendon. I had posters of that guy in my room from when I was fifteen, which was around about the time I knew for absolutely sure I wasn't straight. He was dark-haired, dark-eyed, lithe-built and he had the hottest smile and the sexiest walk I had ever witnessed. I watched his movies endlessly, and each time I saw him I just about burst with longing.

I nodded. "Yes. That's me, sir." I felt nervous but also bursting with excitement. I was really here! After six years on campus, studying acting and even doing a Masters, I was on a film set, and with a job. I was so excited to meet Stuart. I couldn't even imagine what it would be like to finally meet Stuart Glendon face to face.

I had applied for the job of his PA when I saw it on a board at the drama department. I had almost passed out when I saw it – the job of working with Stuart Glendon? Spending time with him, being near him, even talking to him? It didn't seem possible. But it really was real, and when I got an interview for the job – with a member of his team – I had literally run around the room screaming with delight. Not at the interview, that is – in my room before the interview.

"So," Mr. Lawford said. "I'm glad you're here early. Stuart Glendon always likes to start on time."

I swallowed hard. He was really here! Stuart Glendon was here, and I was going to get to meet him. I stared at Mr. Lawford, trying to think of something to say.

"I guess punctuality is important, sir," I said.

I went red. What was I even saying? My poor brain had started to fry from the pressure of being here, on set, waiting for Stuart. In a few moments, I would meet him.

I tried to picture it – I would be briefed and sent to his accommodation, and we'd spend the morning discussing my duties. I would do my best to be polite and listen well, and he'd be friendly and maybe a bit remote. I was ready for that. I wouldn't expect him to like me or even see me, really. After all, I was just his assistant, there to answer his phone and schedule appointments. I didn't think he'd really talk to me much.

"Grand," Mr. Lawford said, grinning. "So, Glendon. This is the guy. Bennet, this is Mr. Stuart Glendon. Glendon, this is Bennet. I guess I'll leave you two to chat."

I stared. A tall man walked into the room. This was him? The man I'd crushed on since I was fifteen? This tall, handsome man in jeans and a shirt, with a tan and black hair just slightly gray at the temples? This was Stuart Glendon? The hottest actor on this planet?

I couldn't even find my voice; I was so honored to meet him.

"Hi, Bennet," he said. I felt my spine tingle at the sound of his words. He had a drawling accent, but a nice, low voice – the resonance of it was rounded and soft and it tingled across my skin just like when I watched one of his movies, except that now, I was next to him. I stared up at him.

He was tall – a head taller than me, at least – and he was broad-chested with a narrow waist and his legs looked like he bicycled twenty miles a day – the muscles were toned and firm and his thighs were corded with muscle, I could see that even through his jeans. He must be in his forties, and he had the most fabulous body I'd ever seen – I could imagine his arms were strong and built and his back would be firm and hard.

He was known to be straight, but I guess it's okay to look, right?

I forgot my manners for a moment, and just stood there. Mr. Lawford laughed.

"I think he's a bit surprised to meet you, Glendon. Sorry...I should have warned him before you walked in."

"Um, no," I said swiftly. I cleared my throat, which felt like it was too tight to breathe properly. "I mean, yes. Yes, I'm pretty surprised. It's a huge honor, Mr. Glendon. Really."

It wasn't at all what I had planned to say. I'd planned to try and be confident; to act like I meet Hollywood stars every day. After all, it was what everyone recommended for an actor's assistant – one should be cool and collected and not thrown by meeting famous individuals.

I was more thrown by meeting this guy than I had been by my final exams or any other scary thing in my life.

He smiled. I thought he had the most beautiful smile in the world. It spread slowly across his face, until last of all the wrinkles formed at the corners of his eyes, which themselves were sparkly. On movies, I thought they were dark brown, but in this moment, they had a hazel cast to them, and seemed almost green. I felt my heart thumping.

He was so gorgeous.

He shrugged. "Well, I guess you should follow me over to where you'll be working."

I swallowed hard. I could barely imagine what this was going to be like. Seeing Stuart Glendon every day for a month, making arrangements for him – which would presumably involve me talking to him – answering his calls…I couldn't bring any image to my mind of what that would be like.

"Yes, sir," I said.

He smiled again, and I thought I was making a fool of myself, because he seemed to be tolerating me rather than actually liking me. I glanced around for Lawford, wanting some kind of indication of what I should do, but he had already started talking to someone else – another guy, big-muscled, carrying a box of camera-equipment. I guessed he was one of the technical experts. I didn't stop to think about it much – I was too busy following Stuart down the pathway.

We went into the street and down, and I saw there were some trailers parked just outside the main street. I felt my heart thump. I was really here! I was following Stuart to his trailer. This was something that, a few years ago, I would never have imagined was possible.

He turned to me.

"Okay," he said. "So. I guess you know what you're doing. Here's the phone whose number everybody has – the director, the producer, the agents…everybody who might need to get hold of me and isn't a friend, has this number. You'll be in charge of this phone. I'm in here, reading through the script. We're going to start shooting in two hours. It's your job to make sure nobody disturbs me while I'm getting ready. Okay?"

"Sure," I said.

I looked at him. He placed a mobile phone in my hands. He stared down at me from the stair – he was a good head taller than me anyway, but on the steps he was two heads taller. I felt a bit foolish. I looked up at him a moment, and when he said nothing, only turned away to go into the trailer, I called him.

"Sir?" I called. "Sorry, sir, but what's the code to unlock the mobile? Just in case I need it?"

He sighed; face pinched in an expression of annoyance. "Look…is it your job to ask me questions, or what?"

I couldn't find my voice for a moment. At first, I was too shocked by his response to say anything, but after a second, my brain kicked in and became rational again. That was unfair. I had to know the PIN. How else was I going to get onto the phone? But, another part of me added, he was right – it wasn't my job to be bothering him; it was my job to avoid other people getting on his case. So, what could I say…?

"Um, maybe," I said.

He looked at me. The expression on his face was wide-eyed, almost disbelieving, and I could almost hear him begging someone to save him from a month with the new assistant. I would have felt hurt, but he had a good face for funny expressions, and even though he was mad at me I just felt honored to be around him.

"Okay, okay," he said. He looked annoyed, but he'd clearly decided to tolerate me. "Where the hell is Tamsyn when you need her? She was my old assistant, and I can tell you that she wouldn't be messing me around like this…"

"Sorry, sir, but I need it."

He ran a hand down his face and I could imagine he was trying to hold in his temper. "Yeah, yeah. You're right," he said. "Here. I'll write that down for you. But don't give it to anybody or lose it, okay..? You never know who might get into that phone."

"Sure," I said.

I waited while he went into the trailer, and I could hear him finding a pen and paper. He was opening drawers and cupboards and his annoyance was evident. He came out a few seconds later, passing me some paper.

"Here," he said. "Now, you go over there somewhere, where you can head off anyone coming this way. I need to be completely undisturbed when I work, okay? Understand that? Completely undisturbed. I'll need an hour to get into character."

"Sure," I said.

That seemed to be the only word I could remember. He looked at me oddly, and I looked back, feeling confused and shy and a little like I wanted to hide. He nodded to me and went into the trailer.

I sat down on the step, the mobile in my hand. I had no idea what I was supposed to do, so I just sat there. I could hear somebody searching around on a table inside the trailer, and I wondered what was going on in there. I studied acting, so I understood very well that he would need an hour undisturbed to get into character. I knew he was a "method actor", and he'd be becoming the person he was portraying.

I wondered about him. I wondered if the person he was portraying – a cowboy, like he usually portrayed – had the taciturn character he now had. I wondered if I would ever get to know the real Stuart Glendon – the actual man, without the covering of a public personality or the characters he acted.

I pushed the thought away. Mainly because it made my heart race and my body heat up with an all-over flush, and because it was silly. I was here, and that should be enough for me.

I deliberately tried to forget about the guy in the trailer behind me – if I thought about him I wouldn't focus – and thought about other things instead. I resorted to watching the street – across from the trailer, some camera guys were gesturing wildly, having some deep conversation I couldn't understand even if I was able to hear, which I couldn't. I sat there and watched them, and then I jumped. The phone was ringing.

I hastily answered.

Chapter 2: Stuart

I sat at the table in the trailer. It was hot, I was tired, and I had an hour to get myself prepared for the first day of filming as Tate Claydon. That was frustrating, to put it mildly. I always liked to have a bit of extra time to get into character, especially on the first day.

"Sir? Sir!" someone called through the door.

"What?" I yelled. Was that my assistant? If it was, he'd better hope he had a super good reason to disturb me. I pushed the door open.

"Sir! Sorry, sir. Phone-call. It's from the director sir."

I stared at him. "You disturbed me for that? What the hell is your job?" I demanded. I wasn't shouting, but I wanted to. I was furious. He must have gathered he'd done something stupid, because the surprised expression left his face.

He went pale.

"Sorry, sir."

"Now, are you going to hand me that phone, or what?" I demanded.

He looked at me. "Should I?" he asked. His eyes were wide; uncertainty all over his expression. "Or should I deal with it..? Only, I thought, seeing it's the director, it might be important, so I didn't answer because I didn't want to say anything and mess it up." He looked down, clearly upset with himself.

I sighed.

"Look. It's your job to answer the phone. Always. No matter who it is. For pity's sake, do I have to tell you what your job is?"

"Yes?" he said. "I mean, I'm not experienced in this, so I guess somebody has to."

I sighed again, louder this time. The most annoying thing was, no matter how hard I tried to get mad at him, I couldn't find any anger. I was just tired out by him. He was maddening, but he was also frustratingly naïve. In the best way. I mean, what was I supposed to say to that?

It kind of was my job to explain how I wanted him to do his job, after all. I just didn't have time.

"Okay," I said. "Look. Your job is this. Hell, do I even have to say this? Your job is: answer my phone. Deal with whatever anyone says. Make appointments for me and remind me about them, and field anything that might concern me that I don't have time to do, like getting the car fixed or making sure I have sandwiches or whatever."

"Okay," he said. He looked hopeful and I drew in a slow, steadying breath.

"Okay. Now, please. Go out there, and do not let anyone disturb me. Anyone. Not the president, not anybody. Okay?"

"Yes, sir."

I shut the door. I slammed it so hard I reckoned it might break off its hinges.

Damn it! Why did he have to break my concentration? I felt like I might have been getting somewhere by now, but he'd just stolen fifteen minutes of mine. Fifteen minutes! It was terrible.

I could have spent those fifteen minutes clearing my mind and settling myself. Now I was going to need fifteen more minutes to do that, which would only leave me half an hour to get into character properly.

I was not going to make the job any easier by getting mad. I tried to calm down, but it was hard.

I went and sat down. I had to get back to my character. I looked around on my desk. I had taken the time to write a backstory for him – some of it was in the movie, some of it wasn't. I read through it, letting my mind reach out, letting myself feel the part. How he walked, how he sat. What made him act like he did.

I couldn't focus. Every time I read anything about Tate, I thought about that new assistant they'd got me. I kept on seeing his face in front of me. It was a nice face, which was the annoying part of it. He had sandy hair, brown eyes and a gently-rounded jaw. He looked like a kind, funny guy, I thought. A friendly, nice person.

Why the hell could he not just do his job?

I leaned back in my chair, trying to forget about the guy. Instead of thinking about Tate and his motives, I kept on thinking of that guy, and trying to decide what could possibly make someone act like that. What the hell did he think he was doing?

Inexperience, I told myself. He's just inexperienced. He said so.

He had no idea what an actor's assistant was supposed to do. Was that so weird? I supposed not, and I supposed that it wasn't so much a mistake on his part as it was on the part of whoever chose him. Why did they not find someone who at least had experience in PA? This guy, I could bet, had never been an assistant to anyone in his life.

I heard a noise outside and I jumped, but it was only someone moving equipment. I was starting to expect him to knock on the door and destroy my concentration.

Somehow, though, no matter how mad I felt, I couldn't sustain it.

I was mad with him, I told myself. I was also just interested in him. Why the hell had he decided to be a PA to an actor when he clearly had no experience in the field? What had gotten into his head at the time?

I took a deep breath and tried to focus on the words on the table in front of me.

Eventually, after a good ten minutes of trying to concentrate, my brain slowly started to focus. I was getting into character, getting the lines and their delivery into my head. It felt good. I felt right. I was starting to feel and think like Tate, to feel the pain in my left hip where it had been injured in a fall from a horse, and the stiff shoulder that I'd had for years, which nevertheless didn't impede me from being frightfully quick with my gun...

"Mr. Glendon?"

"What?" I called. It was a female voice, which was good. If it had been my assistant again, I could not say what I would have done, but it would probably have gotten me a summons. I walked to the door and opened it.

It was Piper, coming to do my makeup. I blinked in surprise. She was the makeup lady and I wasn't expecting that she'd be here for another half hour.

"Am I going to get ready already?" I asked.

"Yes, it is, Mr. Glendon. Sorry to disturb. But you'll need to be ready to go in an hour."

"Okay," I said. "Great." Weirdly, I felt ready. Maybe it was the anger I felt about the assistant. Maybe somehow the anger was actually the missing bit when I had tried to get into Tate's mind. He was mad at everyone! He felt like life had treated him bad, and he was mad at everybody on the face of the earth.

Tate was angry, and I'd been trying to portray him without the anger.

I had actually gotten somewhere! I'd made progress. I felt much better.

"So," I said to the makeup lady. "Let's do this. I'll just need a couple minutes to change. If you can wait outside for five minutes?"

"Sure," she said. "Of course."

I went to where the costume was set out – brown leather trousers, a button-down shirt. I shrugged them on and went to open the door. Fortunately, the clothes were easy to put on. And comfortable, I thought.

"You can come in."

"Oh!" She smiled. "Thanks so much. Great. You look great!" she gushed. "Let's get started on the makeup."

I went to the chair and sat still. I had never liked this part too much – it was a necessary part of acting, but still, I hated the feel of someone else touching my face like that, or fiddling with my hair. I sat back, trying to ignore the flare of irritation that was still there.

I was relieved when, throughout the process of applying makeup, nobody knocked on the door. I was starting to tense, almost waiting for the moment when my assistant would knock and totally disrupt my equilibrium completely. As it happened, it didn't happen. I stood up, the relief weighing almost as much as the tension, and went to the door.

"Right," I said to Piper. "All ready."

"Sure is," she said.

I smiled. I was trying to get into character, and smiling felt weird. I didn't think Tate smiled. Or not often, and not for the sake of propriety and politeness. Tate wouldn't even get what those things were.

I took a deep breath and walked out of the trailer. Almost as soon as I did, I saw him. Bennet Halton, or whatever his name was. He was there, on the horizon by the little house where we would start filming. He was talking to the director.

I took another breath. What the hell was he doing here? He should be somewhere out of the way, with my phone, and not running around all over the place!

I walked up to the house, hoping he wouldn't notice me. If he came over then I would snap back into being Stuart Glendon. I was so deeply in my character, so much Tate so that snapping back into myself would be awful. I went straight into the set.

When I got there uninterrupted by Bennet, I let out a sigh of relief. He hadn't come to bother me! It was wonderful. Again, I was surprised by the amount of relief I felt. It was ridiculous. That guy was starting to become a challenge. If he disrupted me one more time...

"Okay!" The director said, coming in. "We are going to start shooting in about five minutes. Everybody take their positions. We're doing scene one, okay! Scene one."

I stood where I was, on the set. It was just me and Laurie in the first scene, and we were both standing in our positions already. The set was made up so that it was the front room of a house from the eighteen-hundreds. I looked around, and felt that it was Tate and not me, studying the furniture, giving his opinion. He thought it was too fussy.

"And...three, two..." the director counted down. I was already firmly in character, thinking and breathing like Tate.

"Action!"

I looked across at Laurie Montlake. She was wearing period costume, her hair styled like a lady from two hundred years ago. She looked good. I gave her a stern glare, as I was supposed to.

"So?" I asked her. "What did you bring me over here to say?"

I was Tate in this moment, and she saw it, and instantly she was her character too. I could almost see that it wasn't her – Laurie had firm, definite body language. The woman standing in front of me had a hesitant, frightened manner. She was a really good actress, and I felt like we worked well together.

We shot the scene. It went well, and we had it done after two runs, which I thought was impressive. I felt relieved and leaned back against the wall and as I did so I caught sight of somebody wandering around through the camera equipment. Bennet Halton!

"What the hell," I said to him as I came off the set, "are you playing at?"

I was still Tate, my voice gruff and low, and he jumped, as if he'd noticed, then grinned.

"I just thought I'd have a look around, sir. This just seems too cool, being on set."

I felt the anger on my face and he must have seen it, because he stepped back involuntarily.

"Look, this is my place of work," I said. "You don't need to come poking around in here like you're on a summer vacation. It isn't your job to be in here."

"Sorry, sir," he said. "I bumped into the director earlier and he said I could hang around, just for a bit, if I didn't get in the way. I'm really sorry. I know it was dumb, sir. I won't do it again."

I could see how distressed he was and I felt really bad for a moment, realizing how deeply he'd taken it to heart. "Look," I said. "It's okay. Listen, though – when I'm wearing this costume, it's Tate. Not me. And I need to stay in character. If you come over and disturb me, I go snapping back into being me. And that could cost hours and hours of me trying to get back into character. Okay?"

He nodded. "Yeah, sir. I know. I get it."

"Okay," I said.

I went to stand with the other actors – they were also all in character still, and it would make it easier to stay in mine. I had some time before they set up the next scene – we were shooting in the street – and I wanted to stay in character as much as possible until then. I glanced back and Bennet was still there, just in the doorway, talking to a guy who had a tray of coffee.

I felt relieved when I saw him go.

What was wrong with me? I was really furious at Bennet, but part of me liked him. He was so honest, in a way; so eager and ready to learn. I wished I could be more like that. I doubted I was ever so humble.

I turned to Laurie, who was chatting with the other actors. I liked her too, I thought. She was straightforward. I wasn't attracted to her, but then I rarely was attracted to the lead female roles. I admired them and liked them, but it didn't usually happen that attraction built up between us. Her face and figure were beautiful, and I liked her as a person. But I didn't feel any spark with her, not beyond the fact that my character was supposed to be attracted to hers in the movie.

"You had some water or something?" she asked me, gesturing at some bottles that were jumbled on a table nearby.

"Yeah, I did," I said. "So hot today, hey?"

"Yeah," she agreed. It was an unusually hot day. I hadn't had a chance to explore around the town, but I was fairly sure there were no swimming pools nearby. I could really do with a shower. A cold one.

"Okay, guys!" the director called to us. "We're setting up in the street. We'll shoot in about fifteen minutes, okay?"

"Okay," I called back. I had the script with me and I noticed some of the others reading through the copies they had with them. I flipped through my own, thinking that I didn't want to overdo it. The lines had to sound natural.

I followed the guys out into the street. It was sweltering hot outside, and I was dressed in long leather pants. I thought I might pass out in the heat.

When I got there, I spotted Bennet. He was standing some distance from where we would shoot, talking to someone over by the makeshift canteen. I might not have noticed him there if I hadn't been checking to see if he would come and bother me again. I wished that I could go and get something to eat. It was lunchtime and I hadn't had much breakfast. I was starving! I pushed the thought away. It wouldn't take long to shoot this scene – if it went off as well as the first one – and then we could find a meal somewhere.

I found myself wondering about Bennet. He sounded like he knew a bit about acting. I wondered where he came from. He had a neutral accent – definitely American, but it could have been from almost anywhere in the States. I heard footsteps coming over and looked up as the director came out.

I went over to the set, taking up my position with everyone else. I was standing on foot, thankfully, but the other actor was on a horse. I thought that could be problematic. We could take ages shooting this scene.

As it happened, it wasn't too bad. We had to shoot it three or four times, but that was better than what I'd anticipated. By the end of it, I was exhausted.

"I'm going to go and get something to eat," I said to Laurie and Camden Radley, who was playing my brother. They nodded.

"Sure."

I went down towards the canteen, and, just as I settled down with a delicious-looking plate of stew and potatoes, somebody turned up.

"Bennet," I said. I could almost have timed him. "What are you doing here?"

"Nothing, sir," he said. His voice sounded bright. "Just came to the canteen to eat something. It's lunchtime. And I do have the phone, and there haven't been any important phone calls, sir."

I tensed. "Great," I said. "So, you can go and get something to eat."

He looked at me and then turned around, going to the counter. "Sure," he said.

I wondered if he had planned to come and eat with me. I wasn't about to do that – I still had to be Tate, for starters – but still, as he went away I felt strange. I almost wanted him to come and sit here.

"You're being weird," I told myself. He was my assistant, and so annoying! I should be really glad he wasn't bothering me.

I leaned back to see out through the door to see if the others were coming over. I was just stressed, I decided – that was it. Stressed and being driven crazy by a bad assistant. I just needed to relax. It was just stress, playing tricks with my mind and making me feel the need to talk to someone – anyone – even my infuriating personal-assistant.

Chapter 3: Bennet

I walked around the front of the canteen. I had a bag with some sandwiches, but I didn't really feel hungry. I felt confused. I was really trying to do my job, but somehow, Stuart kept on getting mad at me!

I went and found a low wall and sat down on it. It felt weird, being in this town. There were buildings – houses, stores, a station – but all of them were deserted on this side of the town and it felt like this was our town right now. I stayed where I was, watching over the set.

I hadn't hung around to watch Stuart Glendon. Even though I would have wanted to see him, I figured out that he didn't like anyone hanging around. I felt a bit upset. I just wanted to see the man I admired more than any actor ever doing his job! It didn't seem like too much to ask for.

I thought about the morning so far. I'd found out a bit about doing my job – or at least, I should know pretty well by now what Stuart wouldn't handle. He didn't want any interruptions – even from important calls – and he didn't want anybody to disturb him when he was getting ready to shoot a scene.

"I should know that."

I sighed. I had studied acting, after all. I should have realized that was the most basic thing – not wanting to be disturbed, so you could get into character. I did know that, but in the excitement of not wanting to screw up I had forgotten.

"Hey," somebody said. I looked up. A tall guy with big shoulders came over to where I was sitting. He was middle-aged and he looked at me with a friendly smile. "Your first day on set?"

"Yeah," I said. He seemed like a nice guy – friendly and well-meaning – and he came over and sat down beside me on the wall. I moved up a little to make space for him.

"Pretty cool, hey?" he said. He chuckled. He had a sandwich with him too and he bit into it, leaning back against the wall sleepily as he chewed.

"Yeah," I said. So far that was the only word I'd managed to sneak into the conversation. It didn't seem to bother him.

"So, you're working with one of the actors?"

"Yeah," I said.

He grinned. "That's cool. I'm a cameraman. Pretty hot work today. So much sweat I'm surprised I didn't wet the camera." He laughed.

I laughed, too. It was nice to be hanging around with somebody. I'd been feeling pretty lonely today, I had to confess – most of the people I'd talked to had been busy and had only had a second or two to chat before they had to hurry off. This guy was relaxed and I liked that about him already.

"So," he said, pausing to chew his sandwich again. "Which of the actors you work with, then?"

"Stuart Glendon."

"Wow," he said. He sounded impressed. "That's super-cool. He's great. Best actor I've ever seen in a Western movie. Remember "The Fastest Draw in the West"?"

I stared. That was one of my favorites! I grinned. "Sure, I do," I said. "He was amazing, wasn't he?"

He nodded. "Yeah. Great guy."

I leaned back against the wall behind me. "Yeah," I said. "He is." He might be really difficult today, but that didn't mean he wasn't great. I was determined to like him. I was sure that all my mess-ups were things that were really annoying. I had to try to do better.

"I guess I should go get busy again," he said, standing up from where he leaned against the wall. "I guess if they're busy getting ready to shoot, Caz Trenton had better be there."

I smiled. "I'm Bennet," I said. If he'd told me his name, the least I could do is tell him mine also.

"Great," he said. He smiled. He had a nice face – big and friendly. "See you, Bennet. All the best, hey."

"Thanks," I said.

I stood and went back towards the canteen. I didn't know what to do. Stuart seemed to want me to stay as far away as possible, but that didn't make any sense to me. How would I know what he needed me to do if I was hanging out somewhere else?

I stayed near the canteen, and hoped that I would spot him. If he'd already gone off to shoot another scene, I didn't know what to do. I didn't even know how I was supposed to locate him on set!

I felt frustrated. Why was it that nobody had explained to me what my job actually entailed? I mean, the job "actor assistant" seemed to suggest that you hung around with the actor a lot. As it was, this actor didn't want me to be within twenty steps of him, or so it seemed. I stood where I was, leaning on the wall, staring out at the set in the street, where they'd just shot a scene. Maybe they would shoot another one there, I thought. It was already almost one o' clock. I didn't know how many scenes they had to do today or anything.

I was still leaning on the wall when I heard his voice. My boss's. I would recognize his voice anywhere – low and musical and causing a throbbing in my heart.

"So. We're going to shoot another outdoors this afternoon?"

"Yeah. Sorry, Stuart. It's a riding scene. You feeling up for one?"

He chuckled. "You know what I feel about riding, man. We usually end up doing them so many times because I get thrown or fall off or something." He sounded amused, but I thought he was also nervous.

"Yeah. But you won't, you know. You can do it. I know you."

Stuart chuckled. "Yeah, me too. And I know that I will get thrown at least once today, okay?"

The man with him – I recognized him as the producer – was laughing, but I could tell Stuart didn't really think it was funny, even though he was acting as though he did. I wished I could say something, but he wasn't going to listen to me. What could I say to try and reassure him? He was so experienced and talented and I was clearly someone who didn't even know what my job involved.

I sniffed. It was stupid, but it hurt. I stepped back before they saw me and let them go past.

I stood there, waiting until I was sure they couldn't see me. I decided to follow them to the set.

It was my job.

I followed the producer and Stuart, and they went out to a street and stopped. It was a different street to the one where we had filmed the scene where Stuart had been standing and the other actor had been on horseback. It was a street with a railing on one side, and there was an old-fashioned bar across from the railing. I found it so wonderful that the town just happened to have such a cool old bar – none of the set was manufactured. It was all just like it really was.

I focused on Stuart again. He was standing maybe fifteen feet away, diagonally across the street from where I was. He was in costume and somebody came over to touch up his makeup. I watched how his shoulders tensed and I guessed he didn't like people doing his makeup. I was learning a lot about him, in spite of the fact that he didn't seem to want me to.

"Hey! Stuart. You ready?" the other actor called to him. His name was Kenneth Bradfield and I didn't know anything about him, which I suppose was weird, but then I didn't have any interest in any of the other actors. I didn't like him on principle, just because I liked Stuart and I could have wished he was the only person on set.

The man he addressed raised a shoulder, shrugging in a casual way that made my heart race. How could one man be so stunning?

I looked away. It was unreasonable how gorgeous he was and how attracted I was to him. He would never even look at me. He was even straight! Why was I making myself be here and get so close to him?

I guessed that it was because, if I didn't, I would always wish that I'd taken the opportunity to do it.

If I never met him at all, there was no chance at all, I reckoned. At least if I met him, it was that much closer to being possible.

I looked over, distracted, as Stuart walked towards Kenneth.

"Okay," he said. "So, for a start, you're on the ground, right?"

"Yeah. And then I mount up. I'm doing that bit myself. Barry isn't here."

I guessed that Barry was his stunt rider. I wondered who rode for Stuart in his stunts. I couldn't see any sign of anyone else in his costume, so maybe he was going to do it himself. Or maybe there were no stunts for him in this part of the movie.

"Great," Stuart said. I wasn't standing too close – in fact, I couldn't really hear him properly, since he spoke the word quietly. But I could see from his posture that something was making him uncomfortable. I knew from what I'd overheard that he didn't like these bits.

He went over to the side of the road where the bar stood. I stayed where I was. A few moments later, he came out, riding a brown horse. He seemed to be relaxed, and I felt better also.

"We're shooting in three...two...one!" the director shouted. I noticed the camera guys – they had set up on the other side of the road, where the railing was, and I hadn't even seen them arrive and do it. I watched as Stuart rode up the street.

"Hey!" he shouted. Kenneth was leaning on the street-sign near the bar. He was dressed in black and I thought he looked quite convincing. He had his hand in his pocket, and, even though I knew it was acting, when he took out a gun, my heart raced. I wanted to grab it from him. It was stupid, I knew, but I felt protective towards my boss.

"Hey, Tate." Kenneth said in a voice that somehow sounded sinister, even though I couldn't have said why. I had to admit he was a good actor, even though I was here because I thought Stuart was wonderful.

"Henry. What are you doing here?"

Kenneth lifted a shoulder; a casual gesture that fitted the part superbly. "Guess I could ask you the same question."

I was enjoying it, getting involved in the scene. It felt almost like I was watching a Western, except that this one was happening here, in the open air, before me. It was so weird. I could see the cameras and the guys standing around just off-set, but somehow the acting was so strong that it was almost as if I couldn't see those things. All I could see was the two guys, standing in their scene, and it could really have been a shoot-out, even though I could see the cameras and I was standing there myself in the crowd.

"You could," Stuart said mildly. "But then, I'd have to give you an answer. And I'm not sure I want to do that."

I grinned. He was wonderful! He had his gun in his hand, suddenly, and even I hadn't seen how he got it there. He was looking down at Kenneth, and I thought that the way he did it was so beautiful it made my heart race.

"If you say so." Kenneth spoke the lines hard.

I thought they were both wonderful, the way they looked at each other. The tension was so strong that I could have cut it. It really felt like they were about to shoot at each other, and if you had asked me, I would never have thought that they were sitting there holding harmless weapons and that in an hour or two they'd be wearing modern clothes and talking like everyone else.

"So," Stuart said, shifting on horseback. "You going to put that gun down?"

Kenneth raised a brow. "Only if you are."

I held my breath, but at that moment, the horse decided to bolt. I yelled in horror as Stuart clung on, his horse racing down the street. I ran through the crowd, running after them. I could see Stuart was trying to keep on the horse, but it was running and I could see he was having a hard time staying on.

"Stuart!" I screamed, as he was thrown clean off the horse's back.

I didn't stop to think. I ran straight over to him. He was on the ground. He'd hit his head. I could see others walking over, and I instantly found my finger dialing Emergency. They had to get here fast!

"Stuart? Stuart!" I said, patting him on the cheek to check if he was awake. I didn't know what to do – I'd never actually done First Aid, just seen the fire-department guys give us a demonstration when I was at school. I could remember nothing of it, especially not right now.

I was terrified for him.

"Hello?" I said as somebody answered the phone. "Hi! This is Bennet Halton. I'm calling from Oldham. We have an emergency. Stuart Glendon just fell off his horse. He's unconscious."

"Okay, son," the man on the other side of the phone said. "Can you tell me where in Oldham you are?"

"The main street!" I said quickly, looking around. "Outside the bar. We're shooting a movie," I added, just in case he hadn't heard the name of a famous actor and figured that out.

"Oh. Okay, son. Hang on. We'll be there as fast as we can."

I sat next to Stuart. By now, several people had run over. I could see the director. He was standing there, looking helplessly down at the man on the ground. I sat next to Stuart, feeling his pulse, trying to check if he was breathing. He was. He certainly had a pulse, too. It felt so strange to touch him, if I thought about it. I didn't have much time to do any thinking besides checking that he had a pulse and was breathing, though. But he was still unconscious.

"What do we do now?" the other actor asked.

"I don't know, Kenneth," the director said. "Just wait, I guess. This guy called the ambulance." He gestured at me.

"Yes," I said.

Nobody said anything. We were all standing there – except me, who was sitting – and looking at Stuart.

"Should we move him over into the shade?" somebody said.

"No!" I spoke instantly. "No. Don't move him. You're not supposed to move anyone – what if he has a broken neck?"

Nobody said anything else. Nobody else had any comment to make on whether or not that was likely, and, frankly, it was possible. All we knew was that he'd fallen off his horse. Any injury could have resulted. We all waited around. I listened for Stuart's breathing. I had never felt so worried about anyone as I did about him in that moment.

"There they are!" somebody said. The siren of the ambulance. I stayed where I was, crouched by Stuart. An ambulance came up the road, reached the film-set and then carried on part of the way. I stood up, waving to them frantically. They stopped.

"Where is the patient?" the guy driving asked as they neared, his head stuck out of the window to call out. I pointed.

"He's there! He's still unconscious. Please, do something." I was so relieved to see them. The guy nodded and went over and I followed them. I crouched down next to Stuart. Some of the crowd were starting to wander off now. It was just me, the director, and two or three other guys, one of whom was Kenneth. I stayed where I was as the ambulance guys came over to where Stuart was.

"Hey! Hey. Can you hear me?" one of them said. He tapped Stuart on the cheek like I had. They also checked his pulse and breathing.

"He's breathing. He has a heartbeat," the other guy said. I nodded.

"Yes," I said.

The guy gave me a strange look, but nobody told me to get out of the way, and so I stayed where I was. I wasn't going anywhere. I was going to stay next to Stuart all day if I had to.

"What did he fall off?" the guy asked me.

I looked at him like he must be crazy. "A horse," I said. I pointed vaguely in the direction the horse had gone, but somebody must have caught it and taken it back to the stable or wherever it was staying by now, because it wasn't there.

"Okay. How fast was he going?"

"Fast," I said. I felt impatient with the question, but then the other guy decided to at least explain something to me.

"We need to know so we can figure out if he could have a spinal injury."

"Oh." I nodded. "Maybe," I said. I had no idea, but I had seen him fall and it could be that he'd broken something. It had been a really bad fall. I knew my answers were disjointed, but I couldn't help it – it felt like something was stuck in my brain, making it impossible to think straight and causing all my thoughts to come slowly.

We turned our attention back to Stuart. He shifted and coughed.

"Stuart!" I yelled. "You're alive!"

I was grinning and laughing, so happy to see him okay. He opened his eyes, blinking up at me.

"What the hell happened?" he murmured. He tried to shift on the ground, to sit up, but one of the ambulance crew stopped him gently.

"Let me help you up, sir," he said. "You could have broken bones."

"What the hell?" Stuart said, blinking. He looked up at me and I hastily explained.

"You fell off your horse. You hit your head pretty hard. You were unconscious, so I called the ambulance."

"Oh. What...when was this..?" he murmured, and winced, as if he was in pain. He was sitting up, and his hand went to his head. I could see he was in pain and I wasn't surprised. He had hit his head really badly.

"Sir? Do you know your name?" the ambulance guy asked him."

"Um, yeah. Stuart," he said. He spoke slowly and I could see how tired he was.

"And do you know what day it is?" the guy asked.

"Um...Maybe it's Tuesday?" he asked. He looked at me. "Is it Tuesday?"

I grinned and nodded. "Yeah. It is. You're okay!" I exclaimed. I was just so glad he was okay. I could see one of the ambulance guys looking at me weirdly, but I didn't mind. I was just so pleased! To my surprise, Stuart grinned.

"Yeah, I am," he said. "My head sure hurts, though."

I could see that and I looked at the ambulance guys. "Have you got headache pills or something?"

Neither of them answered and Stuart hauled himself upright, swaying. I stood up and grabbed hold of his arm, helping him walk back towards the shade by the buildings. The ambulance guys followed us.

"Sir? You should drink some water."

"Sit down, sir," the other said. "You shouldn't try to stand up yet."

I looked at Stuart. "What do you want to do?" I asked him.

He looked at me and shrugged. "I want to go to sleep, I guess," he said.

"No sleep!" the ambulance guy said instantly. "He's concussed. You need to try and keep him awake."

I looked at the guy. I think he must have seen the expression on my face. I'm not a well-built guy, far from it. But he looked at me wide-eyed and said nothing, and I knew that he had seen the violent look come over me.

I just wanted them to make Stuart better or leave him to recover – not restrict him and bother him and make him have a headache.

"He has to stay awake for a few hours," the other guy said.

I walked with Stuart towards the set. He didn't say anything and I didn't say anything either. I could feel his body pressed against mine and my heart was thumping. I could feel the warmth of his side, and the slight limp he walked with, and the muscle of his shoulder. I had my arm around him, supporting him as he walked. He hadn't said anything about it and I kept it there, face flushed, body flooded with feelings of shyness and pride.

We reached the set and the rest of the film guys crowded around. In that group, the ambulance guys soon ceased bothering us. I saw them talking to the director. I was glad they'd come, but now that Stuart was awake, all I wanted was for him to feel okay and the pain in his head to get better. He was standing leaning against me and the producer came over to talk to him.

"Okay, Glendon?"

"Yeah. I reckon," Stuart said. He stepped a little back, but kept leaning on me. I could sense he felt awkward with my arm around him and so, very reluctantly, I moved it. He stayed beside me.

He was looking at the producer, who was nodding slowly.

"I reckon you should take the afternoon off, Stuart," he said. "Go lie down or whatever. Walk, or whatever you need to do. We'll shoot the remaining scenes tomorrow. Okay?"

"Yeah, I'll do that." He nodded. "I could really do with some time off."

I looked sideways. He looked really tired, I thought. I felt extremely protective towards him. I wasn't going anywhere. I saw him turn to look at me.

"Want to go for a walk?" he asked.

I felt my heart thump. "Yeah!" I said instantly. Then it occurred to me that maybe it would be bad for him to be wandering around. It was a hot day, after all. "Are you sure you can do that?"

He shrugged. "Only one way to find out." He grinned.

I laughed. I felt more wonderful than I could ever have imagined. He trusted me! He liked me. Somehow, there was this weird understanding between us that hadn't been there before. Or, if it had been, I hadn't noticed it, anyway.

"Sure!" I exclaimed.

We walked together down the path away from the set, back towards the trailers. I walked slowly, sensing that Stuart didn't feel at ease on his feet. He didn't say anything and I didn't say anything either – he needed to save his strength. I could see the pain in the tight wrinkles at the corners of his eyes and I knew that he was just not saying how sore it was.

"Thanks," he said as he got to the trailer. "You don't happen to have a headache tablet, do you?"

I shook my head. "I'll get one for you, though," I promised.

He grinned. "Thanks. But hurry back...we're going walking in five minutes."

"Great!" I replied.

Chapter 4: Stuart

I sat in the trailer. It was dark in there, which was good. My head was aching. I lifted my hand to the back of it, just checking that I hadn't broken anything. I could feel a huge lump on my head and I chuckled. It was going to take ages to wear off! It hurt and I sucked in a breath.

"Damn head," I said.

I couldn't really remember what had happened to my head – I could remember being on the set, and then riding...what happened between when I realized my horse was running away and when I woke later, I couldn't remember. I thought about Bennet, and the fact that he had been there when I opened my eyes.

"He's a weird guy," I said to myself.

I smiled. I liked him. I couldn't help it. I'd been feeling like that all day, actually. He was difficult, he was annoying and he had no clue about his job description – at least not when it came to being an assistant to me – but he was a good person. The fact that he was next to me when I came round and was the only person who stayed with me the whole time meant a lot to me.

I wondered if it had been him who called the medical team.

I leaned back. I was tired. Why the hell shouldn't I sleep? They could try staying awake when they had a lump like a damn tomato on their heads! I found a comfortable place and was just starting to fall asleep when somebody knocked on the door.

"Stuart! I'm back! We can go for that walk now. Will you let me in?"

"Okay," I groaned. I stood, stumbled over and opened the door. He stood on the step, grinning cheerfully.

"Here! I even got a cup; just in case you need one." He held up a paper mug like the kind they served coffee in. I smiled.

"Great," I said. "But it's okay, I'll just swallow it down."

I took the headache pill. My fingers brushed his as he passed it to me and I felt the weirdest sensation; a sort of tingle that ran up my arm. That was weird, I thought.

I leaned back, looking at him. He was standing in the doorway, and I thought that he looked great when he smiled. He was a relatively plain guy, I had thought – long, thin face, high cheekbones, honey-brown hair and a long, angular body – but when he smiled, he was really nice-looking. His long face lit up and his eyes were lively.

I blushed. What the hell was I thinking?

My eyes had caught his, and I noticed his widening in surprise. I felt my cheeks redden and swallowed the pill, wincing at the taste.

"You need water," he said.

I rolled my eyes. "I've taken headache pills like this since forever," I said. "If it's going to wear out my stomach-lining, then I already have no stomach lining. Shall we go for this walk, or what?"

He laughed, nodding. "Sure," he said. "That's kind of badass."

"What is? Taking headache pills without water?"

"Yeah."

We both laughed. I fell into step beside him. I wasn't annoyed to have him with me as we walked out towards the set. Far from it – I was glad to have someone with me I trusted. Weirdly, I trusted him. He had shown me already that he wasn't going to walk away and leave me if I needed help.

We walked around the set and up towards the town.

"You had a chance to look round?" I asked him. My head hurt a little less, but being in the sunshine hurt it more. I walked towards the shadow and he followed me. We went towards an old house with a terrace. I leaned against the wall. He stood next to me, about two hands' breadth away. We stood there in the coolness and I shut my eyes, hoping that it would help the pain in my head to lessen.

"No," he said in answer to my question. "Not really."

"Me neither," I agreed. Damn it, why would my head not stop hurting? It had gone off a lot but the injury was still sore, like a tight band was being fastened round my head, the pain centering in my brow just between my eyes.

"It looks like a nice town," Bennet said.

I shrugged. "I don't know. I don't really want to walk around it. I want to go check out the countryside. Want to come with me?"

I opened my eyes again to look at him. He was smiling, and I thought he looked like he really wanted to hang around with me. I couldn't understand that. I'd been a real asshole to him all day. But still, I was glad he was here, helping me.

"Yeah!" he breathed. "Yeah. I'd like that a lot."

"Okay," I said. I felt a pain slam into my head again, as I tried to stand up. I stumbled and he ran over, grabbing my arm, helping me gain my balance.

"You okay, Stuart?" he asked me.

I nodded. "Fine," I said. I stepped away a little. Needing to lean on him felt weird – I didn't want to burden him. He was my assistant, but when it came to actually walking around, I reckoned I didn't need any help. Or I didn't think I should need any help, anyway. I took a step forward.

I almost fell, but walked on. In righting myself, I felt a little better. I walked slowly toward the next building, and the next. There were only a few streets, and then we'd be out of town. Bennet was walking along with me and I glanced back to see him keeping up. I felt pleased that he was there. Annoying he might be, but I didn't want to be on my own when I felt so weird. And Bennet was one of the only people here I trusted to be around me when I was like this.

"So," I said as we walked down the street, heading towards a scrubby, semi-desert landscape beyond the town. "You tend to like getting out of the city?"

He nodded. "Yeah. I grew up in Colorado. Colorado Springs is about two hours from here," he said.

"And that's where you were born?" I asked. I was interested in him. He was difficult to place – neutral accent, no particular mannerisms that suggested any one state above any other.

"Yeah," he agreed. "I lived there my whole life. Never really traveled. You must have traveled loads."

"A bit," I agreed. "Not so much overseas travel, actually. Or not as much as you might think, anyway," I added. I didn't have time when I was working, and when I wasn't working, I wanted to stay at home in California, and enjoy life. I don't actually like traveling much. But I was more interested in finding out about him just then. "You like it here?"

"You mean, here?" he asked. He gestured at the landscape. "Or you mean Colorado in general."

I laughed. "Yeah. I mean Colorado in general."

He shrugged. "I guess," he said. He was silent for a bit and I waited, interested to know what he was going to say. We had walked a bit away from the town, wandering through the dry landscape. I glanced back, just checking that we'd be able to find our way back to the town, should we get lost. It certainly stood out – everything else was pretty flat until one reached the hills on the horizon. "Yeah," he said. "I like it. I grew up here. I guess the place you grew up in always means something to you, right?"

"Yeah," I said.

We stood quietly for a bit. We were just standing out in the hot sunshine. I had put on sunblock, but I didn't know if he had. I felt worried that he would get sunburned – I was already feeling the heat pouring down on me.

"Let's go and stand under that tree," I suggested. "It's so hot out here."

"Yeah," he said. "Good idea."

We went over to the tree. I could feel sweat soaking my forehead and I walked over, the pounding in my head slightly less as we moved into the coolness under the tree. It was a spot with a great view – the landscape stretched endlessly; a space of brown, hard-packed earth and little pebbles, here and there a stand of scrubby grass as the only raised things on a flat, level expanse that stretched to the skyline.

"It's beautiful," he said.

"Yeah," I agreed. I turned to face him. "Pretty much like where you grew up though, hey?"

He shrugged. "More or less," he agreed. "It's not quite this arid around the city. But the landscape is pretty similar, yeah."

I stared out at the landscape. "It's a big sky," I said. It was what I was already starting to love about Colorado – the sky seemed huge here, the blue hugeness of it stretching up endlessly, white clouds towering over the landscape, moving slowly on the breeze. It felt like there was endless room to expand into.

"Yeah," he said. "It's amazing. I feel lucky to have grown up here."

"Must be weird," I said. I had grown up at the coast, in a small town not too far from LA, which was where I lived now. I loved the sea. I couldn't imagine being in a landscape without the ocean being that close.

He chuckled. "Yeah. It is weird, but only if you grew up somewhere else."

I raised a brow, amused by the statement. "Yeah. That's true." That was a new side to him, that playful mocking, I thought. We were standing very close, and he was looking into my eyes in a way that sent warmth radiating through me. I blinked.

I didn't know what I was feeling, but it made my throat tighten.

I made a rasping noise to clear it. He chuckled.

"Hope it's not too dusty out here. Or that the headache pill isn't stuck in your throat."

"Thanks. No, it's not." I made a face. He smiled at me.

We stayed where we were, standing under the tree. I could still feel the strange warmth in my body, and I was still trying to ignore it. At the same time, I wanted to be around him. He interested me.

"You studied in LA?" he asked me.

I nodded. "Yeah. It was a pretty amazing place to study acting." I chuckled, remembering what it had been like. It was a long time ago now, or it felt like it. I looked at Bennet. I guessed he must be at least ten years younger than me. He could have been even younger. I guessed him to be about twenty-six, twenty-seven. "I was so excited when I got my first acting job, straight after studying."

"Really? That's awesome!" he said. "Was that when you were in "All the Stars Over the Sand?"

I raised a brow, nodding. "Yeah! That's right. How did you know?"

He blushed. "I guess I've been a fan of yours for a while now."

"Really?" I looked away. Weirdly, I felt shy. I never normally felt like that, finding out that someone was a fan. But with him, it was different. I guess because we were working with each other. "I didn't think you'd like that kind of movie, oddly."

"You kidding?" it was his turn to be surprised. "No way! I love Westerns. And you're the best Western actor I ever saw. Honestly."

I chuckled. "You think so?" I really felt awkward, but in a good way. I was used to receiving praise – but somehow his praise made me feel shy. I looked away. "I mean, there are some talented guys in Westerns; way more than myself, actually."

He shook his head. "No," he said. "I guess there are good actors, but you have something else. Something special. I'm really sorry I interrupted you this morning."

I blinked again, surprised. I didn't think he had understood why what he'd done had made me so mad at him. "It's okay," I said. "People can make mistakes. It's your first day."

Hell, I thought. Why was I being so reasonable? The guy could have messed up the most important day of shooting. But then, I thought, he'd at least learned fast. And he'd been there when I got hurt; the first on the scene.

"Thanks, Stuart." He sounded really emotional. "I'm glad I didn't mess up your shoot."

I chuckled. "You know, it'll take more than one guy knocking on my door to unsettle me these days."

He grinned. "A bang on the head, maybe?"

I laughed, reaching up to feel how the sore spot felt. It was really tender, but fortunately the headache pills had taken the worst of the soreness away, for the next few hours at least.

He leaned back on the tree next to me and we looked out over the landscape. It really was warm out there, I thought – warm and dry. I was aware of Bennet standing close and I looked out over the surroundings, trying to focus on that instead.

It was weird, I thought, that he had an effect on me. I liked being around him. I enjoyed his company, but in itself that bothered me. I didn't tend to be that approachable with people I barely knew, and I didn't tend to enjoy meeting new people or want to get to know them as quickly as I was getting to know him. I was known for being a real extrovert, but in reality I didn't tend to be that sociable. I tended to take time to get to know people and to be a quieter, more hesitant sort of personality, actually.

"I guess we could either walk for a bit longer, or go back," I said after a long time silent.

He turned to face me, one shoulder lifting in a shrug. "I don't really mind," he said. "It depends on how your head is doing."

I laughed. "My head's okay," I said. It was aching, but considerably less since the headache-pills and it hadn't overpowered them for now. I looked over at him, waiting for him to make a decision about where to go next.

He lifted a shoulder again. "Should we go back?" he asked. "We can always look around the town a bit."

"Okay," I said. "Are there any places still functioning in the town? Or did we take over with the film-set?"

Bennet frowned. "I don't know, Stuart. I had a look around, but I reckon there are a few stores and restaurants still functioning. If you want to go and check it out?"

I raised a brow. "Sounds good to me," I said.

We walked back across the arid landscape towards the town. We were really no more than about five minutes' walk away, but even being that far out made it feel as though we were in another country – it was so much calmer, away from all the hectic work of the set. Even now, as we passed it, camera guys were carrying equipment back from the street, storing it in a trailer for tomorrow.

I walked with Bennet across town, heading towards the one part where we had no scenes to film. It was a newer part of town – though it still looked pretty old-fashioned, to my eye at least – and I caught sight of a bistro. I looked at Bennet.

"You think we can have a drink or something there?" I asked him. For some reason, I really wanted something cold. I guess the pain in my head was made worse by getting overheated, and it was so warm outdoors.

"That'd be great," he said.

I smiled. Bennet had a nice character – he was always so hyped about everything. I really liked that about him. Myself, I tended to be a quieter person; less energized and more cautious. I would never tell anybody that, mind – my public personality was vibrant and up for challenges.

I walked with him to the bistro. It was in a recently-built structure, with big glass windows and a modern-looking plaster facing, but it had kept to the old-fashioned style with a steep roof and a terrace. I instantly liked it. I gestured to the waiter.

"A table for two, please."

"Yes, sir!"

I glanced at Bennet, who was smiling. I thought the waiter recognized me, if his brisk efficiency was anything to indicate anything. I followed him to the table, feeling like Bennet and I shared the secret of my identity. Some of the people in the bistro ignored us, while we had one or two stares. I smiled to myself.

Fame was a weird thing, I thought. I'd never get used to it.

I sat down and Bennet sat down at the table with me. The waiter brought us some menus.

"I could really do with a cold drink," I said. "What about you?" I asked Bennet.

He nodded. "Absolutely."

"We have a selection of hand-brewed lagers?" the waiter said.

My eyes sparkled. Bennet laughed.

While we waited for the drinks, Bennet and I got involved in a discussion about wine. It surprised me that he knew so much about it – since he was younger than me, I had imagined he probably didn't have such a developed taste for such things. But he knew a lot.

"You must have spent a lot of time at wine-tasting," I said.

He chuckled. "Actually, I did. I was part of a society when I was studying."

"Really?" I asked. "You had a wine-tasting society?"

"Absolutely," he said.

We both laughed.

Our drinks arrived, and I took a big sip. It tasted amazing and I gave an appreciative sigh. Bennet chuckled.

"Yeah. It's really good, hey?" he said.

I nodded. "It's wonderful."

We both laughed again. I was surprised by how nice it was to hang out with Bennet. I had really taken against him when we first met, but even then I had noticed how open he was, how resilient, too. He had never actually been thrown by my losing my temper.

"So," I said. "You enjoyed college?"

He shrugged. "It was okay," he said. "I liked it. It was cool to be with people with similar interests to me. You know, people who liked the same subject."

"I guess," I said. I thought back to my own college experience. I hadn't really enjoyed it that much. I was never one for hanging out with people. I tended to keep my own company at college, and if I hung out on the weekend it was to go hiking with a local group.

"You didn't enjoy it so much?" he asked.

"Not really," I admitted. "You know...I'm only saying this to you, but I'm not really the kind of person who gets on easily with others. I guess you must have noticed that this morning, hey?"

He laughed. "No. Really, I did mess up a lot."

I ignored that comment. I still hadn't decided what I thought about that. "I guess I just like more peaceful things. Being in my own home. Taking walks. I've never been much of a sociable type. Not even at college."

"But...but Stuart!" Bennet said. "You have like, a totally party-guy image. I really thought you were pretty social."

I shrugged. "I think people expect that of actors. They expect us to be bold and loud and...I don't know what." I laughed. "But really, I'm not like that. I'm actually quiet."

"I can imagine that," Bennet said, looking at me. I had expected him to be shocked, maybe even a bit less of a fan, if he saw through the public image and down to who I am. But he wasn't. He just smiled and drank his drink. "I like quiet people. They're interesting."

I felt my cheeks redden. "Thanks," I said. I felt shy. Weirdly, it was the first time in a long time that someone had said something nice about me. Not the public personality, not a role. Just myself.

He laughed. "What are the rest of the cast like?" he asked.

I shrugged. "Okay," I said. I didn't want to talk badly of anyone. I wasn't too friendly with Kenneth, who I found a bit exhausting. Laurie was nice – I admired her as an actor. "I like Laurie," I said. "She's a good actor."

"She is," Bennet said. "I mean, from what I've seen of her. I don't really know her – as an actor, I mean."

I smiled. "She's good, as an actor," I said. "I mean...I think she's very professional."

"Do you like her?" he asked.

I laughed. "No. I mean, I like her, but...like, like? Not really."

He looked surprised. I smiled to myself. I wondered what he thought – if my public personality had really gotten everybody as fooled as it had him. I hadn't thought that I had been that convincing. As it was, even if people thought I was constantly hanging out at parties with famous women, I actually wasn't. My own interactions with women hadn't been numerous at all.

"Really?" he said. "Wow. It must be hard to act with her, then."

"It's really easy," I said. "She's really talented and we help each other. I never fall for the leading actresses. I don't tend to fall for people easily. Maybe just because of my past stuff."

He didn't ask me anything. I could see he was listening, and that he wanted to hear what I was talking about, but he didn't try and press me. I wasn't usually this open with people – but the combination of being tired, and the fact that I trusted him, was making it easy to talk to him. I never really got a chance to talk – especially not to people who could accept the real me. I felt he did that.

"I guess I was dumb once – I had a thing with a leading actress. And it was just bad. She was a really difficult person. And, well, I guess it wasn't her fault or mine. It was just horrible."

"I'm sorry," he said.

I laughed. "It's okay. I managed to come through it okay, so I guess I should stop worrying about it. It shouldn't hold me back the way it currently is."

Bennet smiled. "I guess it's not that easy, hey."

I nodded. I didn't say anything for a bit. My head was starting to hurt, but I wasn't really worried about it. I was pleased to be in the coolness of this place, having a drink and talking. I hadn't had a chance to do anything like this in a while.

I sat quietly for a while. Bennet was looking into the street, and I couldn't think of anything to say. I wondered what he was thinking about – his expression was hard to read.

"And you?" I asked.

"And me what?" he asked.

"Nothing." I didn't want to start asking him about his past – we didn't really know each other well enough for that. It was one thing my being expansive about mine – I was tired and he'd asked me about it. But I didn't feel I had the right to pry into his.

I drank another mouthful of my lager. It was pretty strong, and I found myself feeling pretty sleepy. I stretched and stifled a yawn. I noticed Bennet looking at me with a small frown of concern on his brow.

"You okay?" he asked. "I mean, with your head, the guys said you shouldn't sleep and stuff."

"It was about two hours ago, Bennet," I said sleepily. "They didn't say I could never sleep."

He chuckled. "Okay," he said. "I know. I'm being silly. I'm sorry."

I shook my head. He looked upset, and I realized that I'd never really thanked him for what he did. I felt bad. Yeah, I'd said thank you, and it hadn't really been that dangerous, what happened – but if it had been, he would have saved my life. I had to remember that.

"Thank you, by the way," I said slowly. "For what you did earlier. Calling the guys when I fell, and that. It was a big help and I appreciate it."

He looked at me, eyes wide. After a long moment, he found his voice.

"I wanted to help. I was really concerned about you."

"I know," I said. That was what had touched me so much. I might be famous, but I knew better than any how swiftly people can go from thinking everything you do is fantastic to thinking everything you do is terrible – that kind of adulation can so easily turn to censure. But Bennet didn't expect anything of me – he'd not been to shocked by my yelling, even if he had quietly not accepted it. And he'd also not been swayed by my interest. He cared.

I knew how rare that was.

We looked at each other and I felt something in my heart shift. It was weird. In one moment, we were just hanging out together, enjoying each other's company, and then, suddenly, I was feeling something intense inside me, something that settled on my heart and made me look closer, my eyes searching for his.

I blushed and looked away. What the hell? I didn't understand this. I saw Bennet shift uncomfortably. I stood, pushing back my chair. I didn't know what to say. Had I confused him as badly as I was?

I gestured to the front of the space. "I'll pay for the drinks," I said.

"Thanks, Stuart," he said.

I looked at him but he wasn't looking as surprised as he had before. I felt a little worried that he'd noticed that strange thing that happened between us, but he didn't seem to have paid attention. I felt better. I went to the counter.

"Two lagers," I said. "That table there."

I paid the bill – they were surprisingly reasonably-priced – and went to the table.

"I reckon I'm going to go and rest," I said.

"Sure," he agreed.

We walked out of the restaurant and into the warm air of the street. I walked beside him, trying to figure out what just happened. I could only think of one thing – that I was attracted to him. But that wasn't possible. I couldn't believe it. I was confused, and I reckoned the best thing I could do was go and lie down and go to sleep.

I would try and make sense of whatever had happened when I had more energy, even if that took a whole day to achieve. I had to figure out what was happening, and I felt sure that I could, when I felt better tomorrow.

Chapter 5: Bennet

I went back to my accommodation. For the duration of the shoot, I would be staying in a room in one of the houses the film-crew were staying in. I was pleased about that – my room was on the second floor, and it had a view overlooking the wide, beautiful landscape where, a few hours ago, I had stood and talked to Stuart.

I felt my cheeks heat up in a blush, thinking it. I could barely believe it. Weirdly, though, it didn't feel as crazy as I would have expected it to feel. It was natural to be talking to him; it felt like we'd always known each other. I felt my heart flood with warmth just remembering the afternoon.

He was hot and amazing but, also, he was a nice guy.

I smiled. I was sitting on my bed in the accommodation, the door shut and the curtains letting evening light into the room. I thought over the afternoon again and again and I couldn't keep a huge grin off my face. It felt so wonderful to be talking to him, to stand next to him under the tree and just look out over the landscape. I had felt so close to him in that moment, as if our souls could discuss things that I could discuss with nobody else in that shared space.

In the restaurant, too, he'd relaxed a great deal. He had told me about his life – more importantly, he'd told me about his character. It was weird, because I'd never actually thought that he was that much like the public personality the social media portrayed. I had always imagined him to be quiet and laid-back. And he was!

I grinned. It was silly, but I couldn't stop thinking about our conversation and going over all the details again and again. And I could not – absolutely could not – forget that he had looked at me. It was a way I didn't know how to interpret – it had made shivers run down my spine and my heart had thumped. I knew what I thought the look meant.

It wasn't possible.

"No way. Stuart is not showing signs of attraction. Absolutely not."

I pushed the thought away, even though just thinking about it, and just remembering the way he had spoken to me with that sexy voice, made my heart race. I had been sure, as I stared into his impossibly gorgeous dark eyes, that he was looking at me in a particular way. But I couldn't let myself believe that. It wasn't probable.

Stuart could have anybody he wanted.

I stood, going to the window. I looked out over the landscape outside. It was still beautiful, the barren, stony ground stretching towards the distant hills. I remembered standing there with Stuart, looking out across the beautiful, arid landscape.

I felt exhausted. It had been a long day, I realized. It was really early still, just nine o' clock, but I decided to take a shower and go to bed. I went through to the bathroom and stood, letting the hot water sluice over my body, cleaning the dirt off me from the walk and the long afternoon. I looked down at myself. I had a toned body from going for daily jogs. I didn't do a lot of working out, but I tried to do something each day, and I found that it helped a great deal. I thought I didn't look too bad, now that I had to think about it. I blushed, wondering what I looked like to someone who didn't know me.

I imagined Stuart looking at me and my whole body responded. Imagining those dark eyes lingering on my body made me sweat. I turned off the shower and got out, knowing that I really shouldn't be entertaining thoughts like that.

He was so hot and the thought of him being interested in me was easily the most exciting thing I could imagine. I didn't want to get to aroused, though, as I would have to face him for work the next day and I really couldn't focus if I had fallen asleep dreaming of his hands on my body, his kisses pressed to my lips.

I went through to my bedroom and sat down on the bed. I felt better now that I had washed off the dirt from the day's work. I lay down in bed, thinking about what an amazing, full day it was. I had started the day without having met Stuart Glendon, and by the end of it we were already having beers together. It was crazy! I was so happy.

I lay back in the bed and shut my eyes, and I must have been more tired than I realized, because I felt my thoughts drifting and the last thing I noticed just before I slept was that I had remembered to shut the window. I absolutely didn't want insects flying around the room in the middle of the night, keeping me awake.

I woke early the next morning.

Luckily, I tend to wake early, because I hadn't remembered to set my alarm or anything so useful. As it was, though, it was half past seven and the contract agreed that I would meet Stuart at eight each morning to discuss anything he needed to discuss for the day. I ran to the shower, showered again, dried myself and got dressed. I felt weird dressing, and made sure to choose a shirt and a pair of jeans that I knew looked really good. I dried my hair and made sure it was combed and looked clean and dry before running out of the house and down towards the trailers.

"Stuart! Stuart?" I called. I knocked on the door. I thought for a moment that I should go and find him at his accommodation, but I had no idea where the actors were staying. I didn't know if they even stayed in Oldham or if they went to the bigger town nearby to stay in a bigger hotel. I was about to try and find someone who would know where to start looking when someone opened the door.

"Hi. Yes, I'm here. We have an hour before shooting starts. Anything we need to discuss?"

I blinked. I hadn't expected to see him here, much less to see him so wide awake and ready for the day. "Um...yeah," I said. "I mean, sorry, what sort of things?"

He made a face. "Bennet...I mean, is there anything that came up yesterday that I need to know about? Any appointments, or anything scheduled for me in a phone-call?" He looked like he was waiting for me to answer.

"Um, no," I said. That wasn't such a difficult question. I knew the answer to that. There had only been one caller yesterday, and that had been the director and I hadn't answered. I should maybe have called him back, I thought now, but I reckoned that, if he had something to say to Stuart, he would have told him yesterday. I looked at him confidently.

"Good," he said. He sighed. "So. What's your plan for the next hour or two? Mine is to get into character, get into costume, and go shoot the scenes we were supposed to shoot yesterday. What is your job for the next few hours?" He looked at me patiently.

I shrugged. "Hang around here, I guess. Answer the phone, if it rings. Meet you at lunchtime to tell you if there was an important call."

He smiled. "Okay," he said. "You know what? That's pretty efficient, actually. You're getting somewhere."

I stared. "You mean it?" I asked. Then, realizing that was probably a silly thing to ask, I just inclined my head. "Thank you, Stuart."

He raised a brow. "No worries. Now, off you go. I'll know you're around, if you need to tell me anything. But please, wait until I come out of the trailer, okay? I absolutely don't want to be disturbed."

"Okay, great," I said. I went to sit on a bench not too far away from the trailers. It was on the side of the street near where they had shot a scene yesterday. I sat there, listening to the sounds of the film-crew setting up the cameras. That involved a lot of swearing and machines making loud noises. I sat where I was, the phone in my pocket, wondering what Stuart was up to and if I would have a chance to talk with him.

I pushed the thought away. Stuart was busy. He would be even more busy today, given the fact that he had taken the afternoon off yesterday, following his injury. I could only imagine that he wouldn't have a spare minute today. I looked around, watching the director talking to the group of people who were setting the scene.

"Okay, everybody!" he was saying. "We need the cameras there, and there. Come and stand here, Andresen. I need to check something on that screen there."

I watched as they set up. I wondered which scenes they would shoot, since the afternoon scenes would still need to be shot this afternoon. I was amazed by how much making a movie entailed. Having watched a lot of them, I'd never appreciated how much went into it. I wondered what Stuart would think if I succeeded in leaving him in peace this morning.

The hour passed faster than I would have believed possible. I saw Stuart come out of the trailer, dressed in leather trousers, a shirt and a cowboy hat. I couldn't help staring after him as he walked down the path – he had a lithe, strong body and he moved with such easy confidence and grace that I couldn't take my eyes off him.

He reached the bar and I sat where I was, wondering what to do. I had gone on set yesterday and seen how bothered he was by my presence, so I knew that I shouldn't do that again this morning. At the same time, being here and not being close to him was pretty difficult to bear. I didn't want to just sit still and ignore Stuart being here.

I stood and wandered vaguely over towards the set. I didn't plan on going near it, but I just wanted to hang around a bit closer to it and think. I found a wall to sit on and sat there, watching the cameras being moved around and people setting up equipment under a big tent-like structure. I found my mind wandering to thoughts of Stuart; basking in the warmth of his smile and remembering what it had been like to talk to him and spend time alone with him.

I wondered about those looks I sometimes saw on his face; what they meant and if they were really a sign of attraction.

I was still sitting and thinking about that idea when I heard someone come up to sit next to me on the terrace. It was Caz, the cameraman I had spoken to yesterday. He smiled at me.

"Hey. How was your day on the set?"

"Yesterday? It was cool," I said. I considered telling him about Stuart and the accident. I didn't have anyone else to talk to here, and the fact that I didn't really know him actually helped – he couldn't cause me any trouble if he knew my secrets.

"Great," he said. He paused. "How was your boss? The actor guy, that is."

I shrugged. "He's nice," I said. I didn't know how to say anything else. I hadn't got to know the guy well enough to just come out with the fact that I had a crush on Stuart, now that I thought about it. I decided to hold onto that fact for a bit before I divulged it. I would wait and see if a chance arrived to say something.

"I saw you having a drink in the restaurant," he said. "He seems like a distant sort of a guy to me. Not friendly."

I shook my head. "He looks that way, yeah. But when you get to know him, he's actually really friendly. Kind, too," I said.

Caz shrugged. "You can never tell, hey," he said. He grinned at me. "Well, I wish you all the best. If I sit around here I'm going to miss the bit where they need an extra camera. Have a great morning."

I laughed and greeted him, then leaned back against the wall again. I kept on thinking about what he'd said, and about the fact that I now knew Stuart so well. I was sitting lost in thought when the phone rang. I jumped.

"Hello?"

"Hi," a male voice said on the other side of the phone. "I'm Stuart Glendon's agent. Can you schedule a time for him to call me?"

"Okay," I said. I thought about it. "Will lunchtime do? Or can you wait until this evening?"

The man on the other side paused. "It's not urgent," he said. "I can call back at five this evening."

"Okay," I said. "That sounds great. I'll confirm that with Stuart later."

"Thank you," he said.

I thought I wouldn't be able to do this, but, as it happened, that phone-call went really well. I felt pleased with myself. I was leaning back against the wall thinking about it when somebody came over.

"Can you come here a moment, please?"

I looked over at the man. I vaguely recognized him and I didn't recall where I had met him before. "Sure," I replied.

"We need some help with one of the scenes – we need somebody to quickly move some stuff out of the way. I can't spare any of the cameramen – if you could come and help?"

"Oh! Sure," I said again. "I'd be happy to. Where are we moving things?"

"Out in the street," he said. "Just off the road so that we can get the cameras through."

"Okay," I said.

I followed him towards the street. There were a few people moving equipment, but not nearly enough; I saw immediately. There was already a small group of cars and other vehicles waiting to come through and so I hurried to join the rest. I bent to pick up a heavy-looking wooden block – I guessed it was to support something or other – and I carried it away.

I bent to pick up something else, and then I went over to grab another thing. I was hurrying, because I could see the director and the head cameraman coming over, and the actors were following them. Kenneth was leading a horse, and I thought that they needed the space to start shooting. I was trying to be fast, which was why I didn't notice the cable in front of me. I tripped and yelled as I fell.

For a moment, I heard somebody shout my name. Then I crashed down really hard on something and I forgot everything but how painful it was and how much my wrist hurt.

"Bennet?" somebody said. "Bennet. Are you okay?"

I looked up to see two people there. One of them was the cameraman who'd asked me to help with the equipment. The other one was Stuart. I looked up into his eyes, seeing that they were full of concern. I smiled at him, but then I noticed the fresh pain lance up from my arm, which was throbbing and aching.

"I'm okay," I said, trying to grin at him. "I think I can even get up."

I tried to put weight on my arm, but the pain was so bad I almost passed out. I heard Stuart give a shout.

"Can somebody call a doctor or something? Bennet's hurt."

I was lying down, looking up at him, my wrist aching worse than anything I could imagine, and I felt my body tense as Stuart gently touched my arm.

"Where does it hurt?" he asked.

I shut my eyes, his touch traveling up my nerves to my brain and making it fizz with wonderment. It was so exciting, so new. I forgot for a moment about the fact that my arm was in pain and just looked up at him, feeling myself drifting in his beautiful dark eyes.

"I don't think it's that bad," I said.

"Can you see if he can stand?" somebody else called. "The doctor's at the first-aid post."

Stuart ignored whoever had spoken, though I tried to curl my legs up under me and stand. Stuart looked into my eyes, his hand on my shoulder, and gently helped me up.

"Can you stand, Bennet?" he asked me gently. "If you can't I can help you up."

"I will try," I said with a grin. I rolled onto my side, trying to figure out how to get up without putting any weight on my arm. I had to bend my knees to my chest and push up with my one elbow, but I was then kneeling, and able to get my leg out and stand up. I stood where I was, head throbbing.

"Bennet, are you okay?" Stuart asked gently from next to my shoulder. "If you can't stand, just hang onto me, okay?"

I nodded. "I can manage," I said. I was swaying and my arm was throbbing but I was sure I'd be alright. I could certainly stand, and, as soon as I stopped feeling like my head was drifting I would be able to walk in a vague line.

"I'm going to make sure you get to the doctor's," Stuart said.

"Stuart! You can't spare a moment. We have to take this scene at the right time. I need the mid-morning light. Send somebody," the director said.

I looked at Stuart. "I'm fine," I murmured. "Really...you don't have to go with me."

He looked at me and I could see the worry in his eyes. I could feel his hand on my arm, and my heart was throbbing with sheer amazement.

"Okay. But I'm going to come and check on you the moment we finish with the shoots. I'll find you at your accommodation. Okay?"

I swallowed hard. My heart was racing and I could barely believe he said that to me. He really did care. "Okay," I said.

I looked up at him. He was looking back, his brown eyes level and full of worry. I looked away, and somebody else came over.

"Hey," the newly-arrived man said gently. "I know where the first-aid tent is. Can I help you to get there?"

"Thanks," I said. "That would be helpful." I looked back at Stuart, who was watching me with concern. I tried to look confident that I'd be okay, hoping to reassure him. But he still watched us as we walked away.

"You landed really heavily on that arm," the guy who was walking with me said. He was about my age, I reckoned, with a friendly face. I nodded.

"Yeah. It hurts pretty badly. I reckon I might have broken it."

He raised a brow. "Hell. That's bad. Let's get you to the first aid tent and get it checked. Are you a cameraman?" he asked me.

I shook my head, grinning. "I'm an assistant. To Stuart Glendon," I explained. He whistled.

"Wow. That must be pretty hectic stuff."

I laughed. "I guess," I said. "So far it hasn't been. But I guess it could get a bit busier during the month." I winced as we walked over uneven ground. Anything that jolted my arm really hurt. I bent it and cradled my wrist against my chest, the throbbing becoming less frequent now.

We reached a tent. I went in, hoping the guy had some painkillers.

"Doctor?" the man with me said, talking to a shortish man with black hair and hazel eyes who was seated behind a desk. "This guy just fell and hurt his arm. He might have broken it."

"Yes," I said as the doctor stood up and came over. The other guy nodded to me.

"I'll go back to the set."

"Thanks so much," I said sincerely. I couldn't help thinking about the fact that Stuart had insisted that someone go with me. I felt my cheeks flush. He really liked me! I couldn't believe it.

"Okay," the doctor said. "I need to have a look at your arm. Can you tell me where it hurts?"

"My wrist," I said. I winced, reluctantly sitting and letting my arm lie on the table. The doctor bent and very gently touched my wrist. I almost cried with the intense pain that shot up my arm. He nodded.

"Yes, you've cracked something. Of course, I would like to do an x-ray to confirm, but I don't have x-ray equipment here in this tent." He made a face. "So, I'm going to splint it and strap it and then I think the best thing is for you to go to the hospital to have a proper x-ray and get it set properly, if needed."

"Thanks," I said. I felt my heart thump. The nearest hospital was about an hour away, as far as I knew. I wouldn't have to go all the way to Colorado Springs to go to hospital! There must be one in the closer town, where the actors were staying.

He nodded. "Okay. If you can just leave your arm where it is, I'll splint it right away."

I leaned back, trying to ignore the pain in my wrist. My side hurt too, but nothing like the pain that flared down my arm. I winced as the doctor started strapping it tightly between two plastic board-like structures. It felt strangely better when he was done.

"Okay," he said. "I'll get you some painkillers, and Andy will drive you to the hospital. Andy?" he called through the door of the tent.

I nodded to the man who came in. The doctor gave him instructions and I followed him out around the back where there was a small car. I got in, holding my broken arm against my chest – the doctor had put it in a sling, too, but I hung onto it anyway – and we drove to the next town.

The nurse at ER x-rayed my arm, and it was indeed broken. I was exhausted but relieved when, a few hours later, they drove me back to the town with my arm encased in plaster. I went to my accommodation, my heart racing. I knew I was sleepy and my arm still hurt a little even after having taken the painkillers, but I couldn't help feeling warmth flood my chest and feeling wide awake when I thought about the fact that in a few hours I might see Stuart again.

Chapter 6: Stuart

I went to the cameramen's accommodation as soon as I had finished shooting for the day. It was five o'clock in the afternoon, and the sunshine was pouring down rich and warmly over the landscape. I reached the building and paused outside, standing in the long shadow under a tree.

I had no idea what I was doing.

I had been thinking about Bennet most of the day. He had the weirdest effect on me and I couldn't understand what it was. He was good-looking, affable and amusing. I liked his company. I couldn't understand why I felt like I was experiencing more than that.

I liked him.

By that, I thought, with my face red, I meant like liked. In the way people were paying money to see me act like I liked Laurie. But those feelings – the excitement, the longing, the fondness – they were all what I felt for Bennet.

I felt like I was stepping into unknown territory.

I stood there and looked up at the building. Part of me wanted to run away, but part of me wanted to go in. I had promised him I would go in, I told myself. So, I was going to go in. I knew that wasn't really why I was visiting Bennet. I just couldn't admit to myself that I wanted to see him.

I looked up as somebody went out through the door. I took a deep breath and went up, going inside to a big entrance-way. I looked up at the stairs. It was clearly a small hotel, and I had no idea which room Bennet might be in. I went to ask at the reception.

"Which room is Bennet Halton in? Can you call him and tell him Stuart Glendon is here?"

The lady at reception raised a brow. "Of course, sir," she said. "If you'd like to wait here a moment?" she gestured at a couch, glancing at me as I went to sit down. She clearly had seen me in a movie. I appreciated her admiration – I had spent my whole life with people looking at me appreciatively, and I hadn't realized how much I liked it. I also found it draining, though. I sat down on the couch to wait, surprised at how my heart thudded.

She beckoned me over to the desk.

"I told him and he said you should go up. It's room twenty, sir."

"Thank you," I said. I went to the stairs, climbing up to the second floor. I knocked at a door.

"Bennet?" I called. "Hello?"

"Stuart! Hi!" he opened the door. His arm was encased in plaster and I felt my heart flip. He had a frown on his brow, though he was smiling, and I thought he looked surprisingly striking in a green t-shirt I hadn't seen him wearing before.

I felt my heart thud. I could see the tall, thin length of his body, his legs encased in jeans. I could smell him, too – a minty smell like toothpaste. I felt a strange ache in my body and I looked away for a moment, trying to focus again.

"Hi," I said again. "That looks really painful. You broke your arm?"

He chuckled. "Yeah. Pretty dumb, hey. Just the wrist. You fall from a horse and break nothing, and I break my arm tripping on a cable." He was laughing, and I smiled too, but had to disagree.

"You fell directly onto your hand. I saw you. It was a bad fall," I said. "You want to go for a drink, or something?" I asked. In a way, I was really glad to have an excuse to go out with him again. I had really enjoyed it yesterday, if I was honest. I had hoped to be able to find a reason to meet him again today.

"That sounds great," he said, nodding. "I'd love that."

I felt my heart thump. I didn't understand what was happening to me. Well, I did understand, that much was certain. I just hadn't thought I would feel like that for a guy, and especially not for the world's most annoying assistant.

I grinned to myself. Had I ever thought of him like that. I gestured towards the town.

"Shall we go to the same place we went to yesterday?" I asked him.

He nodded. "It's nice," he agreed.

I inclined my head towards the stairs. "Well, then," I said. "When you're ready, let's go."

He shrugged, grabbed a coat from behind the door and followed me to the stairs. I felt my heart thud as he brushed past me on the stairway. My body tingled where it had touched his. I followed him down the stairs, thinking that I should be careful this evening – I really was attracted to him and I didn't want to scare him.

I walked with him through the door and we went towards the bistro from yesterday.

"A table for two?" I asked. The waiter nodded. He was the same waiter from yesterday, perhaps – I had barely noticed him. I hadn't noticed much about the place, I realized as I followed him across the room to a table. It had several windows, and the floor was yellow. Shows how alert I was yesterday, that I missed that, I thought.

I followed Bennet to the table and sat down.

"Same beers as yesterday?"

He nodded. "They were good."

"Great," I said. I sent the waiter to fetch them and leaned back, looking across at Bennet, who smiled at me.

"It's weird, being here again," he said. "I hope your head feels better than it did yesterday."

"Yes, it does. Thanks," I said.

He smiled. "Well, my hand feels a lot better," he said. "It might be the painkillers, though – they're pretty strong."

"Should you have beer?" I asked.

He shrugged. "I can try. If it makes me feel weird, I'll stop. Promise."

I chuckled. "I can't tell you not to, can I?"

"No."

We were both chuckling. It felt so good to know someone I could laugh with; someone who had a gentle sense of humor. I really liked Bennet. I looked up and found him watching me. I stared into his eyes, feeling my heart thud. In that moment, I had felt as though he had been looking at me the same way I had looked at him.

I looked away, my heart thumping.

"Two beers," the waiter said. He put the glasses down on the table, then the bottles, leaving us to pour our own. I did, focusing carefully on it. It gave me a moment's distraction from staring at Bennet and the way the light in the bistro was playing across the shapes of his face.

He had the most stunning mouth ever.

I lifted my beer in salute, hoping – foolishly – that a sip or two would calm me down. I didn't feel any more relaxed when I'd finished drinking. Or, if I did, being more relaxed didn't make me less aware of how confused and wonderful I felt.

He smiled, and I thought there was a questioning look in his smile. I looked back at him, wondering what to say.

"Sorry," I said. "I was trying to remember what you study?"

"I didn't say," Bennet said. "I studied acting. I finished my degree two years ago."

"Really?" I stared. I laughed. "No way! Here, in Colorado? Great stuff!" I smiled at him. I would never have guessed he was into acting. "You know what? I really thought you did accounting."

"No way." He grinned. "I don't know what to say to that." He was laughing, so I knew he was just teasing me. I chuckled.

"I should apologize," I said. "I just figured you were too properly-dressed to be an actor. Acting students usually have style that's a bit more...shall we say...expressive?" I chuckled.

"Absolutely. I guess I've just always been a bit careful about how I dress. Maybe just my background. I don't know. I came from a very proper home. My parents are a teacher and a personal assistant."

"Wow. You made a pretty cool choice, becoming an actor." I was impressed. His parents seemed to me to be quiet conventional people – I didn't know why I thought that, I just kind of figured that from something he'd said. He blushed.

"It wasn't really a difficult choice," he said. "I guess I've just always been fascinated by people and how they think. There's a lot of empathy involved in acting. And in therapy. And there should be in teaching, too." He sounded emphatic.

"Yeah," I said. "I guess I never really thought about it before." I leaned back in my chair, studying him. "But it must have been pretty much a culture shock there?" I asked him. "I mean, guys in acting school are pretty out there."

He smiled. "Well, I'm out there, if you see what I mean. As in, out. If you know what I mean." He looked at me directly, but his expression was relaxed.

"I see!" My voice sounded filled with enthusiasm, even to my own ears, and I hoped he hadn't noticed that. I hadn't thought about it, but one of my main worries about how I felt was that he would be put off by me being interested. I had thought that he was definitely straight – if there were any signs there, subtly put about to let people know – I hadn't seen them.

He raised a brow. "You seem surprised."

"No!" I said quickly. "I mean, yes. Yeah, I am. But not in a rude way. I mean, I think it's great. It's so great that you could come out, and everything." I didn't know what to say. I mean, I couldn't very well tell him that it was one major worry I'd had, and I was so relieved, could I? I blushed and looked away.

He didn't seem to be worried by anything I'd said – he stared across at me peacefully, like he wasn't too bothered by anything we had talked about this evening.

I leaned back in my chair, looking at him. He was looking across at something I couldn't see in the doorway. I studied his face, hoping that I hadn't caused him offense. He kept looking away for a moment or two, and after a bit he looked across at me. I tensed as he asked me a question.

"I guess I feel lucky that my sexuality is my own, to reveal or not as I want to. You must have a hard time, with the press always reporting about your relationships with women?"

I frowned. "You know what the press is like," I said swiftly. "They see you go out for dinner once, and suddenly they want to print stuff all over the place that isn't remotely true. I mean, they probably would print stuff about me and Laurie, because we had lunch together."

"Yeah," he said. "I mean, I guess it must be like that." He sounded halting.

I raised a brow. "Between you and me, Bennet, there haven't been many women I've been interested in." I didn't know why I told him, but I supposed it was because he had done me the honor of being honest with me, and I didn't really feel I could do any less when it came to honesty with him.

"Really?"

I could hear genuine surprise in his voice and I chuckled. "I mean, I'm actually a very relaxed person, like I said yesterday. Trust me, I don't have the energy to get up to half of what the press seems to think I can do."

He laughed. It was a genuine, warm laugh and I felt my body heat up at the sound of it. "Well, that's good to know," he said.

I felt my heart thump. It was a strange statement. I had to wonder why it would be good for him to know. He shrugged, looking at me with an expression that I could only interpret as interest.

It was tempting to touch my foot to his leg, but I didn't know if that was appropriate. I would have done it, but I felt so awkward. This was all new to me. We sat looking at each other across the table. After a moment, he leaned forward and looked into my eyes.

"Shall we leave?" I whispered.

He was close, so much so that I could feel the warm heat of his breath on my face. I could barely breathe myself, and felt my heart thump as he nodded.

"Yes," he said.

I stood and went to the counter to pay the bill, and then, as soon as I had paid it I followed him to the door. He stood next to me on the step, body leaning against mine. I felt a wash of heat through me. It was just starting to go dark and I looked about for somewhere we could go. I was feeling longing running through my body and I was amazed that he seemed to feel it too.

I found myself walking with him towards a shaded corner at the back of the bistro. I looked at him – my height was about a hand's breadth greater than his so I looked down into his eyes. He looked up at me and the message in them was one of as much longing as my own.

Without thinking about it I bent and kissed him, my lips pressed firmly to his. My eyes were shut and I drew his body against mine, his hard, firm strength so delicious in my arms. I could feel his lips under my own, and they were hard too, and so beautiful to kiss. I drew him closer and I heard him give a small gasp. I felt my heart thump.

"Are you sure?" I whispered. "I mean…"

He looked into my eyes. I could see he was smiling, even though his mouth wasn't really tilting upward. "Stuart," he said softly. "How can you possibly think I would not want you?"

I laughed and he laughed.

We went around to the front of the bistro again. I turned to him, feeling impossible desire inside me. "Should we go back?" I asked.

"To my place?" he asked. "Let's, yes."

I let out a breath I hadn't even known I'd been holding.

We walked down the road towards his accommodation and I could barely control the longing as we walked up the stairs outside together. I could feel my heart thudding and I could hardly wait to be there.

Chapter 7: Bennet

I went into my room, hardly able to believe that Stuart followed me. I turned around and looked up at him as he leaned back on the door looking down at me. I felt my heart thump. He looked so handsome and I could see in his body the desire that was rushing through mine.

I took a step forward and he wrapped his arms around me, drawing me tight against him. It felt so strange to be in his arms, and yet so great that I could barely hold back. I pulled him to me, my lips hungry on his, my arms wrapping themselves around him, feeling his strong, hard body against mine.

"I'm sorry," he murmured as he stepped back. He was grinning and I thought he had the most beautiful smile anyone had ever given to anyone on his face. "But, you know, I'm not experienced in this."

I felt my body flood with heat. I smiled. "Well, as it happens, I am."

He laughed. "That helps a lot. I know what I want to do, but I have no idea how to do it."

I chuckled. "Well, I guess we can go ahead and I can tell you how to do something if you get confused." I couldn't believe I was saying that. The reversal of roles between us suddenly felt weird, and it oddly gave me more respect for him, not less. I took a deep breath.

He smiled again. "I guess we could go back to what we were doing just now. I know how to kiss pretty well."

"Yes," I said. "You really do."

His kisses were the most amazing thing I'd ever felt. Their touch was maddeningly soft, but intense at the same time, in a way that set my body on fire and made my heart thump.

He gripped me tight and held me against him and his mouth was hungry on mine. I felt my heart race and he held me close and I couldn't contain my longing anymore. I felt my hands stroke down his back.

He leaned forward and then back, and gently drew me down onto the bed. My heart was thudding so hard I thought it would burst. He reached for me and carefully started to undo my buttons. I felt my body flood with heat as he looked into my eyes.

"You are sure, are you?"

"Of course," I whispered.

He bent to kiss me and I could feel his biceps tight around me, his arms like iron bands holding me so tight against him. My hands moved over his back and then his hands gently tugged at my shirt, moving it back from my shoulders. I could barely breathe as he leaned back, looking at me.

"You're stunning," he said.

I blushed. "I don't have half the looks that you do."

He shook his head, grinning. "You just think that because you've seen my acting-parts."

"No," I said. "I think you're stunning. Not the parts you play."

He looked into my eyes and I felt his body tense as he drew me close, the expression on his face real amazement. I let out a sigh as he pushed me back tenderly against the wall, his hands moving to undo the buttons of my jeans.

I lay back, not expecting that he would want to undress me. It felt different and amazing and my body was aching with longing as he finished. I lay on the bed, naked, and looked up at him.

"So," he said. "I don't really know what to do next." He went red, and I smiled at his shyness fondly.

"Well," I said softly. "I guess I could undress you." I was already standing, and my fingers were moving over his buttons. I was nervous, I realized with surprise. I had spoken confidently, but undressing Stuart felt so weird to me. I looked into his eyes and he smiled back.

"Now what?" he asked.

I stared at him. I couldn't help it. His chest was thick with muscle, his shoulders broad, biceps wide with sinews. I could see how narrow his waist was, how his skin was so soft in the light of the overhead light.

I had slid his jeans down and he sat down to finish the process and I tried not to stare but it was impossible not to. He was so gorgeous and I came and sat down beside him, gently laying my hand on his leg. I felt honored to be sitting here like this. I felt so strange.

"This is me, I guess." He grinned shyly and I put a hand on his chest and looked into his eyes, barely able to contain my longing and the almost fear I felt. I had never felt so strongly about anything or anyone before.

"I guess so," I whispered. I laughed nervously. I knew he was looking to me to explain what to do, but I had never had to do that before. I lay back and gestured to him to join me.

He lay beside me and his lips found mine, eager and firm and his body was big and strong as he pressed against me, his arms holding me tight, his legs against mine, his chest pressed to me. I held him, my hands moving down his back, and gently I moved so that his searching hand could move down lower to my back too.

He sighed and held me close, his lips kissing mine, his hardness so evident where it pressed against me. His hands stroked downwards, finding the cleft between my buttocks, and I gasped as they stroked me there. If he said he had no idea what he was doing, then he must have got an idea from somewhere pretty sharply.

I sighed as his hand moved lower, his fingers stroking the thin skin between my buttocks. I could hardly think. The feelings his touch was calling up were so intense that I didn't even have awareness of my own body anymore except for the skin where his finger stroked so gently and insistently.

I gasped as he carefully pressed, entering me with just the tip of a finger. I hadn't told him to do that – he must have just figured it out for himself, I thought. I could feel my body heating up with longing and I gasped again, louder, as he moved it, back and forth.

"Stuart," I whispered shakily.

I didn't know what to say. He didn't seem to need my help for this part, and I gasped as he carefully moved his finger, gently getting me used to him. I lay where I was and felt him kneel beside me, moving his finger so carefully away that I could barely feel anything.

"Now what?" he whispered.

"I guess you can use something else now," I said. My heart was thudding so fast I could not hear. I couldn't believe I was saying that. He gently knelt behind me and I almost passed out as he slowly rubbed himself across where he had just had his fingers.

I gasped as he rubbed me there again. I had some lubricant in the drawer beside my bed and I got it out, passing it back to him.

"Maybe use this?" I whispered.

"Yeah," he whispered.

I held my breath as I heard him open the bottle and put some in his palm. I felt the cold touch of his fingertip between my buttocks as he gently put some lubricant there too, rubbing it over me in a way that was so arousing I could hardly keep still.

"Okay," he said softly. "I guess I can do what I've been wanting to do for a while now."

I nodded and then felt my breath slow as, so carefully, he pushed into me. I held my breath, expecting it to be painful, since he was really big. But I was relaxed and to my surprise, since he did it so well, I didn't feel any pain. He moved slowly, thrusting into me in a way that rubbed deliciously on the places inside me.

I was panting with longing now, feeling the fullness of him in me, and he moved out and, so carefully, pushed back in again. I sighed and moved against him, moving my body so that instead of feeling a slight pain I felt a delicious pressure in me that was rubbing so perfectly on the spot that was so very good.

I could just hear him over the sounds I was making. He was clearly as aroused as I was and the thought was so exciting that I almost came myself. I had at some stage knelt up and he drew me back against him, his hands on my waist, his body thrusting against mine and I gasped and gasped and then heard him let out a cry. I couldn't contain myself anymore either and I felt my own climax race through me a fraction before his.

He lay down beside me and I collapsed and lay next to him. I could feel my own heart race and I lay beside him and his skin was as soaked with sweat as mine as we just lay there. I could feel his heartbeat beside my ear and I moved against him and he drew me close.

We lay there and I had never felt such an intensity of feeling as I lay beside him.

Chapter 8: Stuart

The sensation of something hard under my cheek was the first thing I noticed. I had been lying beside Bennet, passed out from pleasure. I rolled over sleepily and opened my eyes. I was lying with my head on his shoulder. His arm – the one he'd broken – rested under him, and the other one was thrown out in an abandoned way that made me want to grin.

I sat up, careful not to wake him. He was asleep, eyes gently shut.

I looked down at him. I had never felt anything like this in my life, and I could not stop thinking about it. I recalled the way he gasped as I entered him and how arousing it was, and the way that it had been so exciting to, for once, be the person who had no idea what to do. It made my heart flood with warmth for him.

I remembered what it had felt like to be inside him, the way he had moved against me as I thrust into him, and I felt my cheeks flood with color. It was the best thing and I looked down at him where he slept so softly.

I bent down to him and his eyelids fluttered. He rolled over and I felt my heart flood with a feeling so beautiful I couldn't describe it as I looked at him.

"Sleepy?" I whispered as his eyelids opened slowly. He focused on me and smiled, drawing me close to him.

"A bit," he said. "I always am. I mean, after something like that, and I guess you too."

I smiled. "Not always," I said. I lay down beside him, the feeling of my cum still flooding me, still the most intense and amazing thing. I kissed him.

He sighed and moved closer and I held him, my heart filled with feelings. I kissed him again, more tenderly, and he moved against me and I felt a thrill of longing through me, though it would be hours before I could do anything more than just think.

He lay against me and it felt so natural and good to lie beside him, so much so that I rolled onto my side, the way I always did when I slept, my arm tucked around him and holding him close.

He was sleepy too and he lay against me, his breath a sweet whisper like the sea. I nestled against him and felt my mind drifting. I didn't want to think about anything except how wonderful I felt right now. I was rested and fulfilled and all I wanted to do was lie here with him in my arms and sleep.

I lay there, my mind drifting. I kept on thinking about the evening and I must have dozed again because when I woke up, I could feel my hand was cold and the circulation must have been cut off for a while, because I couldn't move my fingers. I rolled over to get my hand out from between us and Bennet stirred.

"Shh," I said gently. "It's okay. You can sleep."

He sat up and looked at me, a gentle smile on his face. "I guess you need to get back home," he said.

I sighed. "Hotel? Yes. I suppose so," I added, feeling upset. I didn't want to go, but I guessed I had to. He was still grinning at me gently.

"I guess you have to," he said.

"Yeah," I said, resting my hand on his shoulder, and he rested a hand over it, so very gently.

I looked at him and realized that what I was feeling was no longer desire – it was so much more than just that. I could feel it fill my heart and make me smile and I looked into his eyes and knew that this was a special human being, one who meant so much to me.

He smiled back and I felt the warmth in my heart grow.

"I guess I should go," I said quickly. I could hear how rough my voice sounded and I cleared my throat, my emotion making my voice tight. I sat up and he rested a hand on my arm and I turned to look into his eyes.

"You'll get back safely, hey?" Bennet said. He was standing up by the bed and I went and wrapped my arms around him, looking into his eyes.

"Yes," I said. "I will."

I didn't know what to say. I just stood there looking into his eyes, knowing that I would be lying awake thinking of him all night – if I didn't fall asleep the moment I was in bed – and knowing that I couldn't possibly express, to him or anyone else, how I felt right now.

"Sleep well," I whispered.

He smiled and held me close. "I certainly will," he said.

I looked about the room, my clothes in one hand. He pointed towards the bathroom. "The shower's there," he said.

I nodded gratefully and looked at him. He shrugged.

"It's too small for us to both fit."

I laughed. He had read my mind. I went into the bathroom by myself then, and showered, thinking of him and also thinking that it was getting late. I needed to get back pretty soon, but it was nice and warm in the shower and I took some time.

"I'll see you tomorrow," Bennet said as I got out of the shower and went to dress. I nodded.

"Certainly, yes."

He smiled and I drew him against me and I felt that same feeling fill me. I walked to the door and went out and he followed me, pausing in the doorway and squeezing my hand. I looked down at the one that was still bandaged up.

"You look after that arm," I said.

He grinned. "I will."

We looked at each other again and I turned around, hearing the door behind me. I hurried away, thinking about him and wondering if I would ever get to sleep tonight.

I hurried down the stairs. It was empty downstairs except for the lady at the front desk. I was glad that she didn't seem to notice me –

or if she did, she must have assumed I was staying there too, because no surprise registered in her expression. I hurried past and outside.

It was cold out, or cooler than it had been when I arrived. I was glad of my long-sleeved shirt. I grinned, thinking that I should hurry back.

The streets were quiet. It was almost deserted. I looked at my watch and found it was only nine o' clock. I guessed that everyone who was going out was by now firmly ensconced in the pub somewhere. It was probably a good thing, I thought, since then nobody would see me.

I heard two people coming out of a bar somewhere – voices incoherent, rather loud – and I hurried on. I had parked my car just around the corner. I found it and got in, leaning back wearily against the headrest. I chuckled, still totally distracted.

I was thinking about Bennet. I wondered whether he was in bed, and I wished I could have stayed. Something about him made me want to be there.

I drove back to the hotel, the images from the last few hours flooding my mind. It felt so weird to be driving back, and I couldn't really focus. I couldn't describe even to myself how I felt.

I got to the hotel, left my car outside; went in. I nodded to the guy at the front-desk, feeling oddly self-conscious. It wasn't like he could know where I'd just been! I was surprised that I cared, and realized that it wasn't for myself.

I was worried for Bennet.

He didn't need the press.

I had lived for so many years with their invasive presence that I was used to it. But Bennet would be new to all that – and he was innocent. He didn't have the pragmatic mindset that it took to be able to overlook being insulted in newspapers, magazines and social media. He would take it to heart and it would hurt him and that worried me.

I went upstairs to my room and went in, shutting the door behind me. I sat down on the bed, realizing only then that I was exhausted. I hadn't felt so many things in a long time. And it had been a wonderful experience.

I lay down on the bed, my head full of images. I could barely believe what had happened between us, but, now that I thought about it, the feelings had been there for ages. I had felt curious about Bennet the day I met him. And I had to admit that I had liked him perhaps because of his faults and inconsistencies.

I smiled to myself, thinking of him now. He was so stunning, and the feelings that had flooded me when I was with him were utterly different to anything I had experienced before. I stood and got ready for bed, thinking about Bennet and wondering if he was sleeping already.

Oddly enough, the fact that I was attracted to a man didn't worry me. In part, I guess, because I had always understood and accepted other sexualities than straight. I was interested to discover that I was also attracted to guys – to this guy, in particular – but it didn't bother me in the slightest.

I lay back on the pillow and my thoughts wandered and before I was expecting it, they were wandering a little more and I was thinking of Bennet when I lost consciousness.

Chapter 9: Bennet

I woke up with a lovely warm feeling in my chest. I couldn't stop thinking about Stuart, and what had happened the night before. I went to the window and looked out, staring out across the town and looking over at the site where we'd be filming again today. I thought of it as "we" even though I had very little to do with the filming process, but somehow I couldn't help feeling like I was part of everything.

I was still stunned. What had happened yesterday was so unbelievable, and yet it was obviously true. I walked to the chair and picked up my clothes, my mind still running through each precious, amazing memory of the night before and thinking that I felt sleepy and content and wonderful, yet also strangely awake; my entire body refreshed.

I dressed and went down to breakfast half an hour later. There was hardly anybody in the dining-room; most of the cameramen must be already setting up. The shooting would start at nine today. I finished my breakfast and went towards the trailers. I couldn't wait to see Stuart again.

I knocked on the door. It was eight o' clock, and I didn't know if Stuart was there or not. I was surprised to see him walking up from around the corner. I had arrived here before him.

I was about to walk over but his grin washed over me and I had to grin back. I wasn't thinking of anything except how stunning he looked in the sunshine with his big smile making those gorgeous wrinkles at the corners of his eyes. My heart was racing and I couldn't find words.

"Hey," I said carefully.

"Hi to you," Stuart said with a laugh. "Ready for work?"

"I sure am," I said. I felt so shy. I hadn't expected that. I looked over at the bushes a moment, trying to focus myself, and I looked up to find that he was staring at me much the way that I must be staring at him.

"Great," he said. He coughed, clearing his throat as if he, too, felt hesitant and didn't know where to start. He gestured for me to sit down. There was a bench nearby where we usually went to discuss the business of the day. I went and sat down and he joined me. He was sitting a hand's breadth away.

"Okay," he said, clearing his throat. "I guess we have to discuss about the meeting. I'm supposed to have some time with the director. I would like to have it tomorrow. If he approaches you about it, please tell him that. He'll most likely tell me, though, in which case tomorrow afternoon I can't have any appointments. Right..?"

"Yes," I said, nodding. "That's sensible."

"So, if there are any other meetings, schedule them around that, since that's important."

"Great," I said.

We both sounded weird, like we were talking according to a script, and one we hadn't learned. It was automatic and routine, but also halting. We were both completely unsure what to say.

I took notes as we interacted – I always take notes. It's way more reliable than trying to remember things, especially if there might be several things to remember. I saw Stuart grinning at me.

"Is that a college habit?" he asked.

"Yeah," I said. "I always took notes. I think it probably got on the nerves of everybody else, but for me it's good." I was relieved to be able to say something that sounded relaxed.

"For me, too," Stuart said with a smile. "I always think it makes more sense to take notes. There's no way one can remember all that stuff."

"Totally," I agreed.

We both smiled at each other. We were talking, but it was as if we said these things simply for the sake of trying to distract from the fact that we wanted to sit and stare at each other. I felt like I was on fire inside, and I could see in the brightness of his eyes when he looked at me that he felt it too.

The tension was like a taut rope in the air between us.

I cleared my throat. "Sure," I said. "I guess that's everything for the morning."

"Yes," he said, frowning.

We both sat and looked at each other and I could feel the warmth of his gaze and I felt my heart pound. I could feel sweat on my back and I thought it had almost nothing to do with the temperature of the day, which was mild now.

"Would you come into the trailer and have a look at something quickly?" he said to me.

"Yes," I said. I felt my heart skip. We stood and went to the trailer and I followed him in and closed the door. My heart was thudding and I couldn't focus. I had been hoping all morning to talk to him.

"I should not keep you in here too long," he said. "The makeup lady is going to be along soon. I just wanted to say, well, I don't know what to say. I'm stunned." He was smiling. "I don't often run out of words."

I chuckled. "Well, I bet you weren't that lost for words when you were nominated for an Oscar award."

He laughed. "Trust me, I could speak then. But right now, I can't. I honestly don't know what to say about it except that I'm stunned."

"Hopefully not with shock." I was laughing now too, and he shook his head. He reached for my hand and held it.

"No. Honestly, Bennet. I knew there was something that I felt about you when we first met that I'd never felt before."

"Like the most irritated you ever were with anyone?" I offered.

"Yeah, that too," he said. I laughed. "But actually, I think I always felt that there was some special way I felt for you that I'd never felt for anyone." He shook his head. "I don't have words, really."

I blushed. "Me, neither," I said.

We looked at each other and he held my hand and drew me towards him and I looked into his eyes.

"Mr. Glendon? Half an hour before the film-session."

He sighed. "Hey, Piper. You can come in in a moment. I was just in discussion with my assistant."

"Oh, sure!" she called back through the door. "I'll wait a moment then."

I saw him grin and he squeezed my hands and then opened the door, where a young woman with a big suitcase was standing. I nodded to her and she smiled at me in a friendly manner that indicated she had no idea who I was.

"Hey," she said.

"Hi," I greeted.

"Piper, this is my assistant, Bennet. Bennet, that's Piper. She does my makeup, and everybody else's." He sounded cheerful and I smiled.

"Hi, Piper." I greeted.

She nodded to me. "Have a nice day," she called as I walked down the stairs towards the town. I couldn't help my grin as I replied to her.

"I rather will."

I walked on towards the buildings, grinning to myself. I had the phone in my pocket, and I didn't plan to stay too far away from the site where they were doing the filming. I walked on a little and sat down on the wall, watching everybody at the set.

My thoughts drifted in a cloud of recollections of Stuart. I couldn't stop thinking about him. That smile! It was so gorgeous, so playful and bright and fun. I couldn't wait to see him and I hoped he wouldn't mind if I hung around here. Waiting until he came out wouldn't get to his concentration too much, I thought. I stayed where I was.

The phone rang. I took it out, heart thumping. Stuart didn't often get calls and there'd been only a few in the time I'd had the phone, mostly from people who were on set and could have talked to him directly. I answered, wondering who might be calling him at this time of the morning.

"Hello?" the voice on the other side said. It was a male voice and I didn't recognize it as anyone who'd called before. "Is this Stuart Glendon?"

"No," I said. "I'm his personal assistant. If you need to talk to Stuart, you can talk to me and arrange a time. He's shooting a movie right now."

"Right," the man on the other side said uncertainly. "I'm calling from Chandley Medical Center. I am treating Mr. Glendon's cousin. I could not find any other contact for him and so I'm contacting you."

"His cousin?"

"Yes, his cousin, Glen. If it would be possible to tell Mr. Glendon as soon as possible, I would appreciate it. You can contact me on this number with information from him. Thank you."

I didn't know what to say. I went towards the building, not sure if I should tell Stuart now or wait. I had no idea what might be wrong with his cousin and I didn't know if it would be sensible to disturb him when he was working. I hesitated, but I guessed that it would be best to say something. I went over. The set was full of people as usual, the cameramen setting up around and on top of the house where the filming was taking place. I had to slip through the crowd of people on the steps, avoiding cameras and being thrown annoyed glances as I went up towards the door.

"Hello," I murmured as I walked into the house. The one door was open, but the cameramen were mostly blocking it and I squeezed past, feeling desperately out of place. I didn't know how I was going to pass a message to Stuart.

I stood at the back of the room where they were filming. The set was different – this time it was a room with leather chairs and a bar at the back. I saw Kenneth in there, playing the villain. Stuart was leaning on the wall, seemingly unworried but tense – I could see how stiff his pose was and just the sight of it made me get caught up in the scene, wanting to know what was occurring.

I stood where I was, watching the men filming and the director, and I wondered if I could possibly interrupt. I felt there was some urgency to interrupting, but twenty-five people were looking daggers at me, as though they would attack me if I just ran up to the front immediately. I stood where I was, wondering what I was supposed to say.

"Okay!" the director yelled, as Stuart finished a line. "We'll take that one again. Just to be sure. That was great, guys. Kenneth, if you could turn a bit towards me…I feel like the light would be better if it fell on half your face, like that. Yes! Great. Once again."

I seized my opportunity to run forward, just before everybody started up. "Sorry, sir! Sorry," I said to the director, just as he was instructing the cameramen. "I'm Stuart Glendon's PA."

"Yeah, I know," the director said. "What the hell made you come in here, son?" he asked, not unkindly. "We're busy."

I drew a breath. "Sorry," I said. "I just got an important call. From a hospital. I thought he needed to call back."

"And so, you lose us the best part of the lighting for the scene?"

"Yeah," I said.

He sighed. He clearly decided that it would be easier not to fight, and so he shouted to Stuart.

"Hey! Glendon. Your PA says an important phone-call came through for you. Come and chat?"

I watched as Stuart's head shot up and I felt for a moment that he was in character again. I knew it was the case because he was still limping a little as he came over. His character limped. He stood beside me, looking down at me unsurely.

"Who called me?"

"A man from a hospital. He didn't say who he was. I have the number. He said that he's calling about your cousin."

"What?" Stuart went pale. I hadn't guessed it would be someone that close – I had only met my cousins twice in my life, and I barely knew them – but he was shocked. I could see how close he must be to him. "Give me the phone."

I felt relieved that it was important. I had done the right thing. Stuart lifted the phone from my hand and called the number, his face stiff with tension. I watched him walk to the door and I wanted to follow him, but the director was looking at me with a stern face and I guessed it might look weird. It was tricky to stand here and watch, when I just wanted to be able to go over and put my hand on his back and let him know I was here and it was going to be fine.

He was outside for a few minutes. I stood there tensely, wanting to go out there. He appeared again at the door and walked over to me and I felt my heart soar with relief. The director was still standing there and he nodded to him.

"Jaden, I'm sorry. I'm going to have to drive to Boulder."

"What?" the director said. "That's a whole day's drive away, Glendon. I don't know if we can spare that time."

Stuart tensed. "I am driving to Boulder," he said. "My cousin is in hospital."

I looked at the director and I saw him hesitate, realizing that if he didn't do what Stuart said, he would more than likely be making a top film without a top actor. I saw him nod.

"Okay," he said. "You can have three days. But I can't give you more time off, you know."

"Yes!"

I looked at Stuart. He was pale. I wanted to talk to him and find out what was wrong. He looked around the room and looked at the director. "Can I have a minute, please. I need to explain to Bennet."

"Yeah," the director said.

He didn't exactly sound enthusiastic about the idea. I went with Stuart to the door and followed him to where he stood beside a wall. He looked distressed.

"Bennet, that was a doctor from the Medical Center near where my cousin Glen lives. It seems like he had an accident with his bike. It was pretty bad and he wasn't conscious when they brought him in. I have to go up to see him."

"Of course," I said. I could see from how concerned he was that he was clearly much closer to his cousin than I was to mine. He looked worried. I looked up at him, trying to be reassuring.

"I'm fine," he said gently. I could see he wasn't, though. He was clearly affected by it and I walked back with him towards the building, not knowing what to say.

"If I can do something," I said. "I'd be more than happy to."

"For now, it means a lot to me that you called me. Thank you for understanding it was urgent. I'm so grateful I could make this arrangement swiftly."

"Thanks," I said. "I'm glad it was the right thing to do."

"It was," he reassured.

I followed him into the building and he went over to the set. I stood where I was, trying not to get in the way of everybody.

He redid the scene – it took about ten minutes in all – and then the director called to them that they were going to go to film in another building. I followed them out and into the street, walking behind the actors and the director as we all transferred to the bar.

We went in and I had to stand against the wall this time, since there was barely enough floor for the twenty cameramen. I wondered how many people came over at any one time, and guessed that it wasn't very many – they'd have to seat them on the windowsill if more than about twenty people came in at once.

The shooting took until lunchtime. I was tired, and I could only imagine how tired Stuart must be. We went to the canteen together. I was glad when I had a chance to sit with him by myself for a bit.

"It's going to be difficult to go for three days," Stuart said. "I mean, I'm going to have to drive myself there – I will be needing to focus on the driving and I don't even know how long it's going to take. I never did this drive before."

"It's lucky he's so close," I said. "It's not too far away, not for a good car, I suppose."

He looked at me. "I want for you to come with me," he said. "I think it's the perfect solution for me going all that way."

I stared. "You mean it?" I inquired. I was excited and surprised.

"Yes," he said stiffly.

I nodded. "Okay," I said. "I mean, yeah. I'd love to come with you. I really would. I couldn't imagine anything I'd rather spend time on. Really and truly."

He smiled. I felt the warmth, hotter than anything I could imagine, as he grinned at me.

"Okay," he said. "I guess we should get packing. I'll get the car and pick you up tomorrow morning."

I stared. I could barely believe it. We were really doing this.

I spent the day packing, following the crew around when they filmed, and making myself useful lifting cameras and equipment every so often. I couldn't wait for the evening and when I could have supper with Stuart.

We met at the restaurant where we had eaten the other night. I sat down opposite him and felt my heart racing as he sat down too. The waiter came over to take our orders, which was easy enough, since there wasn't too much to choose. I smiled at Stuart, not sure what to say.

"Nervous?" he asked.

"Maybe a little," I said.

He grinned. "Well, I have to admit I am too. I don't know where to start. I've not got much experience in long-distance drives and to be honest, I've never been fond of traveling in cars."

I chuckled. "Luckily, I'm not too bad with them. It was the one bit of fun I used to have as a student – a group of my classmates and I used to do long drives on the weekend, or whenever we had a week off to party. I could organize the stops for us and book hotels."

"You could?" he asked.

I grinned. "I would be happy to."

We sat and talked about other things – the years we'd spent studying, our homes, our experiences at college. I tried to steer away from the topic of the drive, because I could sense how tense it made him. He clearly wasn't kidding about fear of driving.

We spent most of the evening talking and, when we stood to leave, he walked with me to the door and around the corner. I faced him, my heart racing, my body full of the ache for him. He drew me close and looked into my eyes.

"I want you right now," he said softly. "But I don't want to risk oversleeping tomorrow. We need to leave early. I will go sleep at my hotel."

"Okay," I said. I looked into his eyes and I hoped he could see how much I could barely wait to see him tomorrow. He took my hands and held them.

"I'll see you early tomorrow morning. If you could organize the stops for me, that'd be awesome. Thank you."

"I'll see you tomorrow, and I'll do them now," I said.

"Great," he said. "I look forward to seeing you tomorrow."

"Me too."

I leaned forward and he kissed me and I felt the touch of his lips fill me with even more desire and I found it hard to unclasp my arms from around him and feel peaceful again.

"I'll see you tomorrow," he said firmly.

"Yes," I said.

I walked into my hotel a few minutes later, heart racing and body aching with longing. I sat down on my bed to organize the trip and my mind was full of plans for tomorrow and the excitement about it.

Chapter 10: Stuart

I woke up and got out of bed to go to the bathroom. I always wake early without an alarm, if I have to get up early. I don't know why – I guess it's part of having done film shoots at weird times for the last two-dozen years of my life. I am pretty finely-tuned when it comes to waking up.

I showered and dressed, thinking about Bennet. I was glad that he could come along – it would be much easier for me to have someone there to do stuff like organize hotels along the way. And besides, it was going to be so much easier and more-enjoyable for me to have someone with me. Especially someone who mattered.

I couldn't let myself think about my cousin Glen. He was the closest thing I had to family besides my parents. I didn't want to even think about him in danger. I pushed the thought away and walked briskly down to my car.

I drove down the street to the town where we were doing the shoot – for some unknown reason I couldn't think of the name. Probably, I thought with a grin, because it was dark and I hadn't had breakfast or drunk coffee and my head ached. I went into the hotel.

The lady on the desk didn't ask me who I was or what I was doing there and so I went straight up to the room where I had spent most of the night with Bennet.

I knocked on the door. "Hey! Bennet?" I called, trying not to be loud enough to wake everyone in the building. "Are you ready?"

"No," Bennet said with a grin, opening the door.

I laughed. I couldn't help it. I could be serious as anything, but just seeing his face made me laugh. He had a way of lifting my spirits that I appreciated so much.

"Okay," I said. "Have you got your suitcases?" I looked around the room, expecting to see a suitcase somewhere. He gestured to a small case.

"There it is."

"Bennet..." I sighed. "You can't have more than one change of clothes with you."

"Well, we're driving for two of the days. I guess it doesn't matter if I wear the same clothes then, really."

I grinned. "Yeah, I guess not. Come on, let's start driving."

"Yeah!"

We walked down the stairs and past reception and it was possible for me to forget, at least for a moment, that I was going to a hospital. I got into the car and he grinned at me as he got in.

"I organized the hotels for us to stop off at overnight. We should get to the first one by seven o' clock today, if the traffic is anywhere near what it usually is."

I stared and then I laughed. "You know what? That's great."

He grinned. "I guess I had to be able to be a good help somehow."

I shook my head. "Bennet, you are really good for me. Good and helpful and I'm really glad to have you with me."

He looked at me with a big smile and I felt so happy in that moment. I focused on the road, lost in thoughts of what it was going to be like to share a hotel-room with Bennet.

I was still busy driving when it finally lightened enough to be able to see the street-signs. Not that there were any to see – we were on the middle of a national road with wide expanses of bush on either side of us. I looked at Bennet.

"Should we stop for coffee somewhere?"

He raised a brow. "Now that sounds like a wonderful idea," he said. I chuckled.

We drove on, waiting to see when we would reach a gas station. I kept on thinking there was going to be one any moment. He had the phone on his knee, following the route, and he could see the nearest gas-station was about ten minutes away, or so he said.

"Hell. Ten minutes, eh?" I inquired. "I didn't know ten minutes could feel so long."

"It's because you haven't had coffee yet."

We both laughed. Normally I was practically senseless without coffee, but today somehow I seemed to manage, because we pulled up at the correct gas-station and got out.

"Coffee," I said to the attendant at the counter. "Please. Two strong coffees to go. As quick as you can brew them."

The attendant laughed. "Sounds like you've been awake for a long time, sir?"

"Yes."

I was chuckling too as we took our coffees outside. It was a cool morning, the sky radiant blue just touched with white above the hills as we stood and drank. I could smell the smells of oil around us, and the coffee, and the cool breeze. I looked over at the man who stood beside me, leaning against the wall, the cup in his hand.

"Got a long drive ahead. Remind me to stop every four hours."

"I will do," he replied. He sounded compassionate and I was relieved to have him along – I felt safe, weirdly, knowing that he was here with me.

"So," I said as we walked back to the car. "You want anything else for breakfast?" We had bought some muffins too, and I carried them over to the car with us – it was getting a bit too cold out in the breeze.

"No, thanks," he said. "That'll be great."

We sat in the car and ate and I found my thoughts traveling to my cousin. I didn't know what to say. I had been so close to him when I was a kid – he'd lived nearer to us in those days, with my father's brother who had lived just a few streets away. My cousin Glen had been at our house every day. I had seen more of him than of any of my school friends, of whom I hadn't had all that many, and he was the most important person of my own age.

I turned to Bennet.

"Do you have a family?" I asked him. "I mean...uncles, aunts, cousins, that sort of family?"

He shrugged. "I have some cousins. I don't know them too well."

"I see," I said. "Well, I guess I know Glen so well. We grew up together," I explained when I drove. "He was the closest thing to a sibling I had. I was really close to him. When he moved out here, when he was twenty, I really missed him. I try to see him often, but with a career in acting, it's super-hard to be able to plan any real visit."

"I'm sure," he replied. "When did you last visit him?"

"About a year ago," I said. I remembered it so well. "We met at his home and it was great fun. It wasn't my first time here, but I fell in love with this state, I think. I really liked my stay and we had such a great time. We went hiking and chatted a lot."

"It sounds like fun. Great hiking trails there?"

"Absolutely," I said. I wished we were going for longer. I wished he could meet my cousin – always assuming my cousin was able to be met. The guy at the hospital had sounded concerned, and I sure wished that. I drove on, trying not to think about him too much. It was hard to focus if I did so.

We drove all afternoon, barely stopping for longer than ten minutes at a time. By the time we got to the hotel I was completely exhausted. I could barely get up. I was grateful when Bennet did most of the talking – I was tired. Really tired.

I walked up the stairs and when we got to the room I looked around, rather surprised by how nice it was. It was clean and tidy and I even liked it, which was way more than I'd been expecting. I had been hoping for something that wasn't sleeping in a car-seat, and that was pretty much my only expectation. This was much better.

I went through to the bathroom to shower, and Bennet waited at the window. When I came out he turned to me and I sat on the bed.

"I think I might be tired," I said. "But weirdly, I feel like I'm waking up."

Bennet smiled. "I'm going to go and shower," he said.

I watched him go to the shower and felt myself wake up. I could hear the water running in there and I felt my heart racing, wondering what was going on in there and what he was doing. I tried to resist the urge to get up and open the door, knowing that he wouldn't mind if I did, but also knowing that I was happy to sit here and imagine it instead.

I stood up when he came out. He was wearing a towel and I felt like I couldn't ignore him. I walked over and he leaned against me, his skin still warm from the hot shower. I felt my heart thump. I had been exhausted, but weirdly I was completely awake now.

He sat down on the bed beside me and I ran a hand down his back. I was only wearing my shorts too, and I felt that I was overdressed. I rested a hand on his shoulder, looking at him interestedly.

I kissed his neck and he leaned in towards me as I wrapped my arms around him. I could feel the strength in the muscles of his back and, gently, I ran my hand down the back of his neck as I kissed him, feeling how his body relaxed at the touch.

He held me close and I was still kissing him as he ran his hands up my spine, where my shirt would have been if I was wearing one. I felt my heart start to thump and I moved my hands to his chest, looking into his eyes.

"Shall we undress?" My voice was a whisper.

He nodded. I stood and hastily removed my shorts and he removed his towel. When we were naked we sat back down on the bed together. I felt oddly shy; perhaps because we were alone together in a hotel and on a trip that had nothing to do with work. I looked over at him.

"Feeling shy?" he asked.

I nodded. I chuckled. It felt good to admit it. "Yeah."

He was still smiling. "I know. I feel a bit shy, too."

"Really?"

I laughed. I hadn't expected that. Oddly, I'd thought that he was so much more confident in this than I was; that he knew exactly what he was doing and I didn't. It was weird, knowing that he felt it too.

"Well," Bennet murmured. "We can take it slowly."

I swallowed hard. "Yes," I said.

I liked the idea. I reached for him, my arms tightening around him, his chest pressed to mine. Gently I pushed him back onto the bed, and my fingers kneaded his shoulders as he lay down, carefully working the tension out of them. I hadn't realized how much tension was in his shoulders before I actually touched them.

He sighed and rolled over. I laughed under my breath, continuing to work his shoulders, feeling the muscles slowly relax as my hand rubbed over his smooth, fine skin. It felt warm and soft and I liked touching him. It felt good to feel his skin under mine and to hear that I was pleasing him. He was sighing and I liked the sound of his sighs.

I kissed the pale skin between his shoulder-blades and I felt him tense as I did so. I grinned to myself and started to kiss down his spine, feeling the tight muscles next to the spinal column under my lips as I did so. I reached the base of it and gently licked over the very last vertebrae, letting my tongue just gently stray between the tight gluteal muscles.

He sighed again, and I smiled to myself, knowing how good that must feel. I let my finger follow where my tongue had stopped, moving gently between and down to stroke his testes from behind. He gasped and I chuckled, repeating the touch. I tickled him there gently and he gasped again, almost rolling onto his back.

"That tickles."

I laughed and gently stroked his thighs, kneading the tight muscles. I didn't want to make him tense further. I worked on the tight muscles of his thighs, squeezing them gently with my fingers until I felt them start to relax. It took longer than I would have thought. Then I started to move on to the gluteal muscles, kneading them.

He sighed and I could feel how relaxed he was. I gently let my finger stray between them again, touching him so gently, making him sigh and rub against me more insistently. I smiled to myself and reached into the bedside drawer for lubricant – I was used to where it was, now, and carefully coated my hands with it, warming it a little between my palms. I rubbed it on his skin and he sighed again as I carefully started to push inside.

I felt him tense a little and so I went more slowly, feeling his body relax again as my finger slid into him. It felt tight and I gently moved my finger, trying to help him relax without rushing him. My other hand was still stroking his back, marveling at the firm muscles of his body as I did so. I felt him relax further and slowly, so carefully, slid in another finger. He sighed and this time I could feel he was ready.

I was certainly ready too. I was thick and stiff with arousal, my shaft firm as I gently pressed against him. I pushed in, going as slowly as I could, not wanting to hurt him in any way. He gasped and I tensed, not sure yet if I should pull out or push in further. I felt almost too good to want to pull out, but if he needed me to I would.

He didn't say anything as I pushed in further, no sounds of pain or distress, and so I gently pulled partly out and pushed in again, feeling like streaks of fire were running down my veins and pulsing through my body with each motion. It felt tight and warm and wonderful.

I moved slowly, not wanting to rush this, enjoying each sensation, each rub against me as I went in and pulled out and repeated the motion again and again. He was gasping now too, and I changed the angle slightly, hoping to find a spot that gave him as much enjoyment as I was feeling too.

I found something, because I heard an overwhelmed sound in his voice and so I kept that angle, pushing in and out, rubbing all the places that felt as good in him as they did for me, making him cry out with longing as I moved in him, hearing him start to groan with satisfaction in a way that perfectly matched how I felt, making me get closer and closer to my climax and move faster and faster.

I cried out as I, too, felt a flood of sensation so intense that I felt my body contract and then, as suddenly, relax. Complete relaxation flooded me and I lay down, my breath gasping as my brain was flooded with a fulfilment so intense I couldn't think.

I lay against him, feeling the bliss spread through my body as I slowly came back to my senses. I lay there for a while and then rolled off him and lay beside him, wrapping my arm around him and holding him close.

He lay in my arms and I felt a feeling that was even more beautiful filling my heart as he rested his head on the pillow beside mine. I kissed his cheek and he opened his eyes and kissed me sleepily, then moved so that his head was on my shoulder. I stroked his hair and felt something flood me – an impossible tenderness that I had never felt before. He was still smiling a little in his sleep and I thought that I loved him – his annoying, innocent, good-natured and caring self. I loved him so much. I was still thinking about that as my brain drifted into sleep.

Chapter 11: Bennet

I slipped out of bed and stood at the side of it, looking at Stuart where he slept. I didn't want to wake him and so I tiptoed to the shower. My mind was flooded with thoughts of how we had been together.

I went to shower, feeling the warm water sluice down my body. It felt good and I relaxed further. I thought that we didn't have to rush today. We could sleep for a relatively long time this morning. At least, I could let the driver sleep, I thought. It was important that he stayed awake.

I went and sat in the chair. I looked out of the window, looking out across the small town where we'd stopped for the night. I could see the roofs of the houses, mostly steep and tiled, reaching to the hills, where the sky was pale with the morning. I sat there, not really thinking about anything, just enjoying the space where I could sit and not think about anything.

"Bennet?" I heard someone say.

I went over to where Stuart was waking. I sat down beside him, kissing his hair. He opened his eyes and smiled.

"Good morning," he said. "You're awake early."

"I don't think we have to be," I said softly. "You can sleep if you want to. We don't have to rush today."

He shook his head. "I don't mind waking up if you're awake."

I smiled and looked into his eyes. He looked so half-asleep and I longed to get into bed and sleep beside him for another hour. He smiled at me.

"I think I could sleep for another half an hour," he said.

I nodded. "Me, too."

I lay down beside him and almost as soon as I had, I felt my own thoughts shift sleepily. I woke to feel him sitting up. He rested a hand on the back of mine.

"I guess we should get up," he said.

I nodded. "Yeah, I suppose," I agreed. "I reckon we have to get moving."

"Yes," he agreed. He went to the shower and it was my turn to sit outside and I found myself imagining him in there. I wanted to open the door.

He came out a few minutes later, washed and fresh and wrapped in a towel. He dressed really quickly – I was amazed by the fact that he'd brought fresh jeans. I was just going to wear the same trousers all day that I'd worn yesterday, and tomorrow. He dressed carefully, and sat down.

"Should we go to breakfast?" he offered.

I looked at him. "If it won't hold up the journey too long," I said carefully. I knew he was desperate to get to his cousin, to whom he seemed to be very close.

Stuart shrugged. "I think we can spare an extra half an hour for a sit-down breakfast."

I nodded. "Great," I said.

We went downstairs and I felt acutely conscious of how gorgeous he looked. He was wearing fresh jeans and a shirt and I was aware of his body close to mine. I sat down opposite him, feeling shy for some reason as we sat down there in the quiet, coffee-scented room.

"Coffee, sir?" the waiter asked. Stuart grinned.

"As much as you have, please."

The waiter laughed and I smiled to myself, thanking the man as he poured coffee for me too. We sat there in the silence of the room and I looked around, thinking that I was just so at peace in this moment.

"I want to try and get to Glen after breakfast," Stuart said.

"Great," I replied. "I think it's about another hour before we get into Boulder. From there, it shouldn't be too hard to find the medical center, right?"

He nodded. "I'm sure we can find it. I'm so grateful for that thing." He patted the phone where I'd put it on the table so I could hear it ring.

I chuckled. "Yeah."

We finished breakfast in silence – there was a choice of toast, cereal or some home-baked buns. I had a bit of everything. We went down to the car and Stuart got into the driver's seat.

"I can drive," I said.

He looked at my broken arm. "I think it'd be better if I do," he said.

I chuckled. "Yeah," I said again.

He got in and we drove towards the town. It took about an hour, and I was expecting to doze off, but oddly I didn't.

We reached the margins of the city in the early morning. I could feel that Stuart was tense as we drove in – he was sitting straight at the wheel and I could see him staring out at the place, not really thinking about anything except the hospital and how to get there.

We followed the instructions on the phone – I did my best to navigate, and Stuart listened, looking out through the window, not saying anything as I told him the instructions from the screen. We arrived at eight o'clock which was, apparently, the beginning of visitor's rounds.

"Let's go in," Stuart said.

We hurried to the reception desk. We were met by a woman in a white uniform who gave us both a stern look. She didn't seem to recognize Stuart, which could only mean that she didn't have any taste in movies – in my opinion at least.

"Mr. Glendon?" she said as he showed his identification. "Your cousin is in the intensive care. Doctor Muller will be here shortly. He will take you to see him."

"Thank you," Stuart replied. I could see how tense he was and I wished the guy would just hurry up, so that we could see his cousin. Didn't they understand how painful it was, how worried he must be, just standing around?

I looked around me, watching white-coated people walking, listening to the sound of someone polishing the floor nearby and sitting with Stuart, feeling his tension through the stiff way his hand held mine.

Eventually, a man in a white coat turned up. We had been sitting on some chairs, just waiting. He looked around and then came over. I thought that maybe he recognized him.

"Mr. Glendon?" he greeted. "Your cousin is awake. He is in satisfactory condition and I believe that tomorrow we'll move him to a general ward. Please, follow me upstairs."

We followed the doctor to the ICU. I looked at Stuart, who looked at the doctor.

"Can we go in together?" he asked.

"Usually, no," the doctor said. "But since Mr. Glendon is recovered so well, I can make an exception and let you both in."

"Thank you," Stuart said.

I felt relieved. I had been so worried about the fact that Stuart would have to go in alone and I wanted to be there. I smiled gratefully at the doctor and followed them into the ward.

I looked at the man on the bed. In a weird way, I instantly saw Stuart. He had a square jaw and a longish face, like Stuart, but he had softer features than Stuart and seemed older. He looked at his cousin, unable to focus for a moment. Then he saw who it was and grinned.

"Stuart Glendon? What the hell are you doing here..?" he exclaimed it joyfully. The doctor looked worried and went over to check his drip-line, but Stuart bent down to hug him, heedless of the monitors or the stern face of the doctor looking at him.

"Of course, I came," he said. "I had to see you Glen. What did you do to yourself, hey? I'm so glad they called me."

"I got beat pretty bad when I fell," he said. He gestured to his leg. "So many broken bones. Leg, arm, ribs...I don't even know how many broken bones I got."

"Lots, by the look of things," Stuart chuckled. I could see the care on his face and I stepped back, giving both of them some space to talk.

I didn't think that Glen had noticed me yet and so I stayed where I was, trying to give them both time on their own.

"I guess. I reckon the doctor will move me out of here now. I damn well hope he does. Monitors and stuff keep on going...I can't find a moment to think in here."

Stuart laughed. "I can believe it's really frustrating."

Glen nodded. "Yeah." His eyes turned to me and he looked at Stuart, who was standing close to me. "Who's that?" he asked.

Stuart smiled, looking over at me with his eyes full of warmth. "My assistant, Bennet Halford," he said. He was standing close to me and even though we weren't touching, I think it was clear how we felt.

"Assistant, hey?" Glen looked at Stuart suspiciously. "That's what you call it now, is it?" His tone was scorn-filled.

I could tell that he was guessing something, and that his guess was going to be right. I was surprised by the fact that I felt embarrassed. I had never actually felt embarrassed about who I am before, and the shock of that made me angry.

"Cousin...I hope you didn't mean that as I took it," Stuart said carefully. I could hear the anger in his voice, but maybe somebody who didn't know him wouldn't know how close he was to hitting someone. It was anger like the heat from a fire.

"You know how I meant it," his cousin said. He wasn't looking at us anymore and the hurt I felt almost moved me to tears. I had never been treated with such indifference before.

I looked at Stuart. He looked at me and I thought he could tell the hurt that I was feeling, because he rested a hand on my arm.

"It's okay," he said to me. He looked back at his cousin. "I don't know what to say," he said tightly. "I'll leave you to rest. I don't want to fight with you because you're ill. I'm going to go and talk to the doctor now. I'm sure he'll let you know when you can be discharged from this place."

"I sure hope he does." Glen said. He seemed angry and I felt my cheeks burn. I just wanted to get out of this ward and away from this man as quickly as possible.

I followed him to the door. The doctor, who had been in the ward all that time, followed us out. I didn't want him to see how angry I was, or to treat either of us condescendingly, so I walked to the other side of the hallway.

"...yes, we can come and fetch him tomorrow if he's ready to go home," Stuart said. "And organize a lift home for when he is ready, if not then."

"And will you be able to collect him next week?"

"I'm only in town today and tomorrow," Stuart explained.

I stayed where I was, feeling that weird sense of insult that had hurt so deeply even though so much of it had just been implied, not actually said. I looked out of the window, watching the sunshine tentatively wash across the gray concrete. It was a cold day and the street was dark, the tall buildings around us making a grid across the clouds. I felt tired, suddenly, and confused.

"Hey," Stuart said softly, coming up and tapping my arm. "Come on. We can go now."

I felt so weary that I just had the energy to nod, following him out of the building.

We reached the outdoors and stood on the sidewalk. There was a big parking-lot and an area with grass and a bench. Stuart wandered toward the grass.

"I'm sorry about that," he said. "I wasn't expecting it."

I shook my head. "It's okay," I said. "I don't need your family to accept me."

I was hurt, and I spoke out of hurt and he looked at me crossly. "I do," he said.

I swallowed hard. Weirdly, that made all the difference. "Okay," I said.

He ran a hand down his face. "You know, I'm really tired. I reckon I'd like to go and lie down. What do you think about finding that hotel you booked for us?"

I tried to find neutral words, but I wanted to talk about what had happened. "Okay," I said again. "I'll go check the booking." I scrolled through to find them. I wasn't talking about what had happened.

Stuart nodded when I showed him. "I'll drive there," he said.

I could tell I was going to have to say something but I couldn't think of where to start. I felt hurt but I didn't know what to say about it because I knew that if I was insulted, then I was effectively insulting his cousin, who meant a lot to him.

But at the same time, I felt like I mattered to him. I didn't think that I meant nothing. I knew that he didn't think badly of me the way that I felt everyone did by now. I sat in the car beside him and looked out of the window and said nothing all the way to the hotel.

When we got inside, Stuart turned to me. "Bennet," he said gently.

"What?" I asked. I didn't want to talk to him. I felt like I didn't want to stay in this place anymore. It was ridiculous how much such a little thing had hurt, but it had and I would be lying if I denied it. I had never had anybody look away from me, as if they couldn't even bear their gaze to rest on me.

"Bennet... my cousin was unacceptably rude. I would have done more were he not very injured. I guess he thinks he knows me and part of it is finding out that there's something he doesn't know about me."

"If he doesn't know that about you then he doesn't know you very well."

"That's not true – I didn't know that about myself either, and I know myself well." Stuart laughed.

"I don't find that amusing," I said.

He sighed. "Hell, you could try to, though."

I looked at him. I felt hurt and angry and I didn't know what to say. I stood and went to the window, trying to ignore the pain in my heart.

Was I supposed to just ignore the way that guy looked at me? Ignore the fact that nobody had ever insulted me for who I am before, until his cousin?

I stood where I was, looking out at the scene.

I felt too angry to speak to him and I knew it was silly of me – after all, he hadn't done anything that had caused me so much pain. His cousin had, and that wasn't even vaguely his fault. But what could I say?

I looked out over the city, and my mind wandered to what I would have felt like if Stuart had defended me. If he'd caused a scene, it would just have distressed his cousin. I knew that was why he hadn't said something.

"I'm going to go to bed for a while," Stuart murmured. He went to the bathroom and I heard him shut the door and go into the shower. I didn't even turn to look at the room. I barely had taken a moment to study it. It was painted a sort of creamy color, with white bedlinen. That was all I knew about it.

I stared out of the window, not really thinking or feeling anything. I was in shock, I thought. I had been so insulted and hurt that it was almost as if somebody had assaulted me. I heard him open the door again about five minutes later and come out, followed by a sweet smell of body-wash that made my own body ache. I wanted him so much. I stood there ignoring him and looking out of the window. It occurred to me after being there for five minutes that I was being silly.

Here he was, lying in bed not three paces away, and I was standing here and staring out of the window, ignoring him. I was being stupid. I went over to the bed and sat down.

"I know why you did what you did," I said softly. "I know that if you'd started arguing with your cousin, it might have harmed him."

Stuart had his eyes closed and I thought that he might be asleep. I waited for him to say something, and when he didn't say anything I coughed.

"Stuart," I said softly, when he'd lain there a moment. "I know you didn't mean your cousin to insult me. I know you are not ashamed."

At that, he sat up. I could see the distress in his eyes when he reached for me. I felt his strong arms wrap around me and he held me close, my chest embraced by his strong arms and his head resting on my shoulder.

"I could not risk arguing with him, you're right," he said softly. "But I need you to know something. I am never ashamed of you. I want the whole world to know I'm with you. I don't know how I'm going to do that, but I'm going to have to, because I don't want to keep you a secret. You matter to me so much and I want that anybody who meets me, knows about that."

I let out a sigh. I hadn't realized how much it had hurt, and now that he said that, I felt tears on my cheeks. I held him close, then looked up at him firmly.

"Stuart," I said. "I am really touched. Truly, I am. But I can't let you risk your reputation. You matter to me, too, you know. And if you think it would be damaging to your career to let people know, well, then I think it would be better to hide."

"No," he said. He was sitting next to me and I was shocked by the strength of his tone. He sounded angry and it took me a second to note that he wasn't angry with anyone present. "No. I am not going to hide this about myself. I am not going to hide you. I might have to think about the best way to come out, but I know we can figure something out."

I let out a sigh. I hadn't realized until now how much it had upset me, or that I was thinking that he would hide me; that he would have to, because somehow I would be a burden on his career. I held him and he held me and we sat there quietly, both of us with so much to think on.

After a moment he leaned back and sighed. "I guess we can sleep for a while, hey?" he said. "It's only ten o'clock, and the next visiting-hours are at four, I think. So, we have today pretty much to ourselves."

"Good," I said.

Suddenly the idea of being here with him in a hotel room seemed more appealing. I went to the shower and washed myself, my soul singing with excitement. I hadn't realized how much I had come to be fond of Stuart, or how he had come to value me too. I walked out of the shower and across the five paces to the bed.

"I don't know if I'm sleepy," I said as I got in under the cover beside him. I was naked and so was he. I lay down and snuggled against him.

He turned around and smiled at me, a slow smile that made my heart thud swiftly in my chest.

"I didn't think I had energy. But apparently I do."

I sighed as he drew me against him, holding me close. His mouth was insistent on mine and I felt my body melt against his as he held me tight to his muscular self.

I felt his hands stroking my back and I shut my eyes, knowing that I wanted him with every ounce of my body. I kissed him and his hand gently stroked my shoulder and I lay beside him, feeling better than I had felt for many days.

Chapter 12: Stuart

I slipped out of bed and tiptoed across the room. It was early afternoon, and I felt refreshed as I realized we must have slept for about an hour. I glanced back to where Bennet slept, his brownish hair on the pillow, standing out in contrast with the pale room around.

I stood in the doorway, thinking that I was so lucky to have him in my life. He was gentle and funny and caring and helpful and amusing...I grinned at myself in the mirror.

I hadn't realized just how much I felt for him and how much he had come to mean to me in these last few days. Not until I finally had to confront it and think about it. I knew that I wanted to tell everybody how I felt.

I made up a plan of action as I got dressed. I would contact my press people and get them to think of something. I knew that my image had been very bad-boyish, but I also felt that, with thought behind the PR, it might be made even more appealing if I suddenly came out.

I shook my head at myself. It was ridiculous that I was even thinking like that. I wished that I lived in a time when it was possible for an actor just to be themselves. I mean, the job description did imply that I spent large portions of my life being somebody besides myself, but it would be nice to live in a time when, offstage, I got to be who I really am.

It was time to start.

I walked lightly back to the bed and sat down on it, thinking that I might not wake Bennet, but the moment the bed creaked he fluttered his eyelids.

"Is that you?" he murmured.

"No."

We both laughed. He sat up and I took his hand. He looked tired and I smiled to myself, thinking that I loved him so much in every way

I saw him, but especially when he woke, looking around as if unsure of where he was.

"Is it midday?" he asked.

I nodded. "It is indeed. I reckon it's lunchtime. I, for one, am pretty hungry."

He grinned. "I could really do with a sandwich or something."

I smiled. "I'm sure we can do better than that. Will you help me to look for a restaurant?"

He chuckled. "I'd be pleased to. I guess I can complain that it isn't fair that I always get to choose them, but I suppose it's your job to complain."

"Which I won't, because I'm more than happy to leave that sort of choice to you."

"Thank you."

We both laughed. I watched as he got out of bed, stretching to pick up his shirt and trousers where he'd left them on the chair beside the bed. While he dressed, I searched my phone for the number of my press guy. I found it and decided to discuss with Bennet. Any coming out I was going to do, he would have to be part of.

Besides, I thought as we settled down beside each other, he was the one with more experience than me about this. If anybody could help me to know what to do and how to do it regarding coming-out, it would be him. I sat with him and waited while I looked on my phone for things to do and he searched for places like restaurants.

"Okay," he said. "I found one. They do artisanal local products, and traditional fare."

"Sounds amazing," I said. "You know...how did you know that would be my choice, if I was picking somewhere?" It was exactly the kind of food I liked best. I could barely believe he knew me so well – almost better than I did.

He chuckled. "I don't know. You struck me as a guy who likes being at home and cooking meals and family. You kind of seem family-oriented and the kind of person who likes well-made things."

I laughed. "You know, I know people who have known me for my whole life who don't know me that well."

He shrugged. "I guess something I can do is notice things."

I smiled. I was really touched. I hadn't thought that anybody could know me that well, never mind after a few days of knowing. I looked at him surprised.

"You are really observant, you know. I guess you haven't considered acting full-time?"

"Me?" He chuckled. "No. I really don't think I'm that good at it." He tilted his head, considering. "I mean, I think the bit that got me was the study of acting itself, not actually doing it."

I shook my head, looking at him thoughtfully. I knew what he meant, but at the same time I couldn't agree with him. I could tell what would be good qualities for an actor. "I disagree, you know. I mean, you can clearly watch people and think about what makes them do what they do. And you have insight into characters. I think you could be a really good actor, if you wanted."

He looked away, seeming embarrassed, though I thought the idea appealed. "I don't know really," he said. "But if you say it, I guess I can't argue, can I?"

"I don't know…it might be quite fun to discuss. But I know what you mean."

We both laughed and he took my hand, his dark eyes sparkling and making me think that it might not be a plan to go out to lunch – maybe we should just stay here instead.

He looked up at me and I could tell that he knew what I was thinking.

"I think we should go to that restaurant – they shut at four o' clock, and re-open at seven."

"Oh. Hell. Well, then. I guess we should go. But I intend to come back here immediately afterward."

He smiled and I knew that he knew exactly what I was thinking. He was still smiling as we went down the hall and to the front door, ready to go off to lunch together.

I looked down at the bed where my cousin lay. I didn't know what to say. He looked peaceful, and I didn't want to disturb him. I was glad to see him in another ward – it felt better to talk to him without all the equipment and computers blinking and disturbing us.

I was glad to have a chance to speak to him by himself. I could understand that he had difficulty understanding what was going on, but at the same time I really hoped I could make him, because if he didn't accept me it would hurt a lot. I cared for him and he was the closest thing to family – besides my parents – that I had. If I was somehow unacceptable, it would be hard for me to carry on being who I am.

"Hey," I said.

"Hey, Stuart," Glendon said. He sounded more like himself than he had in the intensive-care. I thought he was more relaxed here in this ward, and that might mean it was easier to talk to him, too. I tried to say something, but he got in before I could do so. "Stuart...I overreacted earlier."

I didn't know what to say. "Thank you for saying so," I said.

He chuckled. "I was really rude and I am really sorry. It was just a surprise, that's all." He laughed again, quite softly. "I reckon I grew up thinking you were the guy all the girls wanted – I grew up a bit in your shadow. And so, when I discovered that wasn't entirely who you are, I found that so much of me had been built around thinking that, it was hard to understand."

I was surprised. "You felt like the girls noticed me?"

He chuckled. "Stuart, you mean you never noticed? Half the girls at school were trying to get noticed by you. You never really seemed to care about it, and I always thought it was because you knew and you were just jaded by it all. Like, you knew how stunning you are so you couldn't bother about those girls."

I laughed. "No way. You might have actually made it clear to me what was happening. I really did never pay any attention. I guess there were some girls I liked, but besides them, I didn't notice anybody."

My cousin coughed. "Stuart...you're just so difficult, you know that?"

I sat down on the chair by the bed. He was smiling but he looked so tired and I felt concerned for him. I knew that the doctor was taking good care of him and that he would be able to go home, but I wished that I could do more for him. "I know," I said. "But really...I feel like all of the confusion inside me has resolved. I feel like I know who I am."

"Good," my cousin said.

I looked into his eyes – a few shades paler than mine, and I felt my heart melt when he took my hand and held it in his for a moment.

"Stuart," he said. "I have always felt close to you. And I really am sorry I reacted so badly. I am proud of you, and I always will be. You're my best friend and your being more you only makes it easier to like you."

I swallowed hard. I couldn't have hoped for somebody to say something nicer. It was hard not to get teary and so I looked down, trying to find my voice.

"Thanks," I said. "You know, that means the world to me."

He grinned. "Well, I'm glad to hear it."

We both chuckled. I sat there beside him, thinking it was really peaceful here and I hadn't noticed before. With the monitor gone, the ward was silent, and the window was open letting in a cool scent from the street far below. I felt at peace sitting here with him. He looked much better than he had and I thought he looked relaxed too, as if we were both happier now we'd talked.

"I'm glad you told me." My cousin seemed calmer than he'd seemed even when I first came in. "I would have felt terrible if I found out later."

I smiled. "I'm glad I told you," I said. "I mean, anything more encouraging than what you said would be hard to find." I squeezed his hand, feeling touched. "It really helped me, by the way."

He shrugged. "I'm just glad you trust me."

I let out a sigh. I was surprised I ever doubted him. I hadn't really considered what I thought his reaction would be; just told him without much thought because there wasn't any other explanation to give. I was glad that happened, since now I could think a bit harder about how I was going to address the issue with the press and with the rest of my relatives.

We sat there and I felt my phone resting against my leg. It must be getting late, I realized – I was feeling tired and hungry and I could almost sense that Bennet must be hungry. I stood.

"I should go," I said to my cousin. "If there is absolutely any help you need with anything, please call me straightaway. And I mean absolutely anything."

He chuckled. "Thanks, Stuart."

I went to the door, feeling my heart twist. I had become used to him being injured, but seeing him like this still bothered me. I looked forward to when he would be at home and he would have freedom again. I had always hated hospitals, feeling like they incarcerated people. I would be happy to come up and visit him again as soon as the movie was made.

I walked down the hallway to where Bennet was waiting. I went to him and took his hand. "He's okay," I murmured as he held me close. I supposed that my comment wasn't too clear – I mean, we both knew he was physically okay, or he wouldn't have been moved to the general ward – but I meant he was okay again with us.

Bennet held me tight and wordlessly and I leaned against him, feeling safe and good when he held me. I felt strange inside – more like

I could be here with him, more like I was accepted and that it was okay to be me. It was silly – I mean, in some way I never felt like I couldn't be – but having acceptance from one member of my family, especially one who meant so much, meant the world to me.

"Shall we go downstairs?" he asked.

I nodded. "Yeah," I said. "Let's go home."

We went downstairs and out of the big front doors, walking silently across the tiles and out into the evening. It felt good to be outside and I drew in a few deep breaths, walking across to the car where we'd parked it a few feet away.

"Is it time for supper?"

Bennet chuckled. "It's only five o'clock."

I smiled. "Well, for some strange reason, I'm starving. Shall we go to a restaurant and have something small and a drink?"

Bennet grinned. "I'd really like to," he said. He took out his phone.

I drove according to directions.

We drove up to an expensive-looking spot.

"I don't know if this is the sort of thing you were thinking of, but it was close and I guessed it would fit your taste."

I laughed. "Yes, Bennet, you are absolutely right," I said. I looked at it and looked at him and I couldn't stop myself from drawing him against me and holding him close. I was so pleased we'd told someone and I couldn't wait to tell more people – both those in my family and everybody in the press. I really felt like it was time, finally, to be myself; who I really am.

We went into the restaurant together and it felt like we were finally acknowledging who we are, what our true nature was. I hadn't ever felt self-conscious about it before, but now, with my cousin's words still loud in my ears, I felt absolutely comfortable and absolutely right being there with Bennet.

We let the waiter show us to a table for two, and I sat down opposite him, feeling like some tension I hadn't even known I had been carrying was slowly sliding off my shoulders. I looked up to find Bennet watching me. He had opened the menu but he was looking at me with a big smile on his face that made my heart glow.

"You look really stunning when you think, you know."

I laughed. "I guess you better appreciate it – it's a rare occurrence."

We both laughed and I looked down at the menu again, studying it. The wine-list was extensive, the food fancy. I might be wealthy – or have come into wealth during my life – but I have never had expensive taste in food and it never developed. I still like good, home-made fare. I looked across at Bennet, the look a question all in itself.

"I reckon we can get a side-dish to share and some wine?" He must have guessed what was in my head, because that sounded perfect to me.

"That's excellent," I said.

We placed our orders – I was impressed by Bennet's taste – and we sat there and waited for them to arrive. I looked over at him, feeling warmth flood my heart, watching him where he sat with his head tipped to one side, the light in the room warm on his brown hair.

"Bennet?" I said softly.

"Yes, Stuart?" he said sleepily. I thought he sounded relaxed and like a weight had gone from his shoulders, too. I smiled at him warmly.

"I just wanted to say it's so good to be here with you. I'm so glad that you found me, or I found you, or that we found each other."

He grinned. "Me, too."

The waiter brought our drinks but I think neither of us noticed him. We were both looking across the table at each other, and I felt such warmth in my heart and knew I couldn't wait until the reply from my press advisers tomorrow.

Chapter 13: Bennet

I was in the shower early the next morning. I usually hate waking up early, but this morning I woke full of energy after spending the night in Stuart's arms. I was relaxed and strangely energized and I almost sang in the shower, except for the fact that Stuart was in the bedroom and I didn't want to scare him too much.

I came out to find him dressing. He turned and smiled as I came over to reach for my own clothes, which were lying on the chair. He looked like he'd slept well, too; even though it was still not quite light outside the windows.

"I'm looking forward to having access to the set, actually."

"Me, too," I said. It felt strange, thinking about being there. Big cities were what I was used to, and the tiny town was – though different to my expectations – actually something I missed. I wanted to go there.

"It's going to be weird being back at work, though." He smiled at me. I knew what he meant – I had so enjoyed a day with him without having to do anything – just having time to talk, and relax, and get to know each other a little more. I had found out so much about him in that time and, even though we had to visit his cousin twice that day, we had seen more of each other than we usually got to on set.

"It is."

He chuckled. "It's just as well I have you dealing with all the administrative stuff – I'd go crazy without that, you know."

"Thanks," I said. I appreciated that. I had felt like I wasn't any use at first. It was good to know he did have use for what I did. I could imagine it was helpful – after all, how was he supposed to be Tate Claydon if he was busy making appointments as himself?

He went to the door and I followed him, going out into the well-lit corridor together. We went to reception – we'd already paid the bill yesterday evening to make it faster today – and then out to the car. We drove off before it was fully morning, and I felt myself start to sleep as we went on.

I woke up at around nine o' clock. I blinked, looking around. We were stopped on the side of the road, and Stuart was on a call. That surprised me, since all calls were supposed to come to the phone he'd given me. But clearly some people had his personal number.

"Yes, Gerald. Yes, I know. Yeah...I accept that. But you know I have to do this. We can't exactly just not be seen."

I felt tension hit me and looked out of the window, watching the bushes at the roadside and the bright sunshine on the distant land. I didn't want to listen and hear how hard it was for the press-agent to accept me. I didn't want to think about the fact that he must think I shouldn't be known about.

"I will call back later. Okay? Let me know if you have a plan."

I looked around as Stuart turned to me. He didn't look angry – rather, his expression was clear, his eyes lit with a focus I hadn't seen there before.

"We are going to stop for lunch at about midday, hey?" he asked as he stepped on the pedal and sent us onto the road.

"Yeah," I said. I hesitated to ask him what had been said, since I felt that, if he wasn't telling me, there must be some reason for his not doing so.

He started talking about it as soon as we were driving, however. "I was just talking to the press guy," he said. "And he seems to think there's a pretty easy way to get out that I'm not straight. He reckons he can make a great press-release about it that'll actually boost my image. He said he'd contact me later to discuss."

"He thinks so?" I was surprised. I hadn't expected that at all.

"Absolutely," Stuart said. "I mean, it doesn't surprise me."

"Really?"

I looked at him. I was completely flabbergasted, and he chuckled.

"Bennet." He said it gently. "Did you really think that it would ruin my career?"

"I was worried," I admitted. I looked at the windshield, not making eye-contact with him. I had really been concerned, thinking that his entire reputation was based on the fact that he was straight. He looked at me sideways and I had to laugh.

"Bennet," he said carefully. "I'm a good actor. A very good actor. It shouldn't matter to people if I'm straight or not and, in this current time, I don't think it does."

"Yeah," I said. "Sorry. I should have known that."

He shook his head. "No," he said. "No, I didn't mean that. I didn't mean you to feel bad for thinking that, really I didn't. I don't blame you for worrying. But I know it's just fine."

We were silent and the only sound in the car was the rumble of trucks on the road outside. The engine itself was extremely quiet – it was an Audi sports car and I had to admit it was really amazing. I looked around, too awake now to drop off to sleep.

We drove for most of the day – except for occasional stops for coffee and for lunch – and then at around three, he got another call. We were on the road and he pulled off to answer it.

"Hi? Gerard?" he answered. I listened to his voice and tried not to focus on the conversation, but I felt stressed by the fact that his tone was neutral. I looked out at the street, watching the way the bushes waved in the breeze and trying to focus on the late-afternoon glow that filled the skies.

"Okay," he said. He turned to me. "I don't know what you'd think about this, but Gerard wants to meet us for a photo-session sometime next week." He looked at me with a frown, as if he wasn't sure of his response.

"Photo-session?" I stared. I felt a mix of terror and elation. I'd would never have even imagined being in a magazine, ever.

"Yeah," Stuart said. "Sorry. I know. I told him you wouldn't like that. I won't say anything if you say you don't want to."

I was still staring at him. "He wants me to be in a photo-session. A photo-session with you." I still couldn't believe it.

"Yes," he said. He was chuckling now. "Why not? It's way better that we represent ourselves the way we want than if the press takes some photos of us that could compromise us."

"Absolutely," I said. I was still in shock, I think, my brain working excessively slowly. All I could think about was the fact that I was going to be photographed with Stuart and featured in a magazine. It was like a strange dream – and not an entirely unscary one as I am really scared of publicity. Even being in the college newspaper once had been terrifying for me.

Stuart looked at me. "You okay..?"

I nodded. "Yeah, just a bit scared, actually. I mean, I've never even been photographed before. Except for once, in the newspaper for the college. And even that was pretty weird."

He chuckled. "Well, as long as you're okay with it, I'll tell him yes, we're going to do that."

I let out a breath. I hadn't realized how worried I'd been; how much the whole thing had stressed me. He was still grinning as we drove on. I felt my eyelids grow heavy and I was soon finding myself falling asleep.

We stayed in the hotel I'd booked and I fell asleep again in Stuart's arms.

I woke later than him, hearing him in the shower. It was seven o' clock, and it felt luxurious to be in bed after all the traveling we'd been doing in the last few days. I lay there, just thinking and letting my mind drift. It was so strange how my life had changed in the past few weeks. Strange and amazing, I thought to myself. I had never thought I'd get the job when I applied to be Stuart's assistant and I still didn't even understand why I'd done it. I guess because I'd fallen for him ten years ago and he had always been somebody important to me.

I slipped out of bed and went to the chair, searching for my trousers. I couldn't remember where I'd put them last night. I heard Stuart come out of the shower behind me and looked up to see him grinning at me.

"Good morning," he said.

I laughed. He was looking at me longingly and I felt my face flood with heat. I wanted him so much in that moment and he came to me and wrapped his arms around me, drawing me down to the bed.

"Stuart," I said softly, as his hands ran down my naked skin, making my body tingle all over. "We need to drive."

He kissed my hair up near my ear, his mouth moving lower, to my neck, and then sat up, eyes glinting brightly.

"We don't have to go for another half an hour at least," he said. He pushed me lightly and I flopped onto my back and then he lay down beside me, kissing me again.

It was more than an hour later when we finally were ready to head for the town. As it happened, I thought, it wasn't a problem. We had four hours to get there, which meant we'd be there by midday. We hadn't said we'd be exactly three days away, and I reckoned the director would just have to find a way to reschedule a few extra hours here and there.

We didn't talk much on the last part of the drive. We were both wrapped up in our thoughts, I think, and I was speechless with excitement about the photo-session and the whole thought of getting back to Oldham. It was weird, but I actually liked it there – even though it was really small.

"Stuart!" the director greeted us, when we finally turned up at the small town. It was half-past twelve, and I was starving. I stood behind Stuart, the phone in my pocket, trying not to get in the way of anybody. Stuart shook the man's hand and seemed glad to be back too; and the director asked him about the trip, his health and his cousin, in that order.

"We're all fine," Stuart said. "When are we going to be filming the next section?"

"Today at five," the director said. "I was expecting you. We saved up the evening scenes to be shot today. You might be working quite late."

"Sure," he said.

I grinned at him as we both went towards the restaurant. The director had eventually let us go, and we wandered towards our usual place, ready to get something to eat.

"I didn't mention the photo-session yet," Stuart said. "I don't want him to think I'll miss filming for another day."

"Yeah," I agreed. "I'm sure there'll be a good time to mention it."

"I'm sure, too."

We both sat in the restaurant, looking through the menu – just to check if there was anything we hadn't already tried – and lost in our own thoughts. I couldn't stop thinking about how wonderful it was that I didn't have to stay hidden.

I was nervous and excited and I didn't even know what I thought about all that was happening. I looked around the restaurant and thought that I was so pleased to be back in Oldham and it was the best possible place – small and familiar – to be in when so many big things were happening.

Chapter 14: Stuart

I woke up early in the hotel. I rolled over and looked down at Bennet as I tried to sneak out of the bed, knowing that he would almost inevitably wake up. I grinned as his eyes fluttered and he stared up at me, his own pale brown eyes so striking that I couldn't help my smile broadening as I looked down at him.

"Good morning," I said.

He smiled and sat up, long pale arms – including the one in the cast – resting on the covers. "Good morning."

I sat down beside him. "I can never sneak out of bed without waking you," I observed jokingly.

He chuckled. "That's not true. You sneaked to the shower when we were in the hotel – I woke up when you were in there."

"That's true," I replied. "But usually you wake up first."

"Yeah."

We both smiled at each other and I felt my heart fill with light. It was just so nice to be here with him, to wake up early and know we were going to work together the whole day. I was looking forward to hearing more from Gerard, too – he had said he'd get back to me today about the photo-shoot. I still had to tell our director when it was going to happen.

I went to the shower and then got dressed, listening to the birdsong outside. Even in the one day we'd spent in Boulder in the town center I'd stopped being used to that.

I dressed and, when Stuart came out of the shower, we went down to breakfast together. Since we got back I'd stopped wanting to hide away from people. We were going to release our photos soon and I knew there were no press people here – the camera-guys were all trustworthy, or they would have already sold compromising photos of all of us by now.

When I got to the set, about two hours later, we were all ready to shoot. It had been an exhausting session the previous day, and I was surprised that I had plenty of energy today. I would have expected to be completely worn-out, but, as it happened, I could hardly wait to be there.

"You're early, Glendon," the director commented. It was hard to tell what he was thinking, or if he was tired or not – he always had the same closed expression. I nodded.

"I am. I can't wait to get started," I said honestly.

He gave me a smile, which was almost more daunting than his usual look. "Great," he said.

I went over to join the other actors on the set. Laurie was there, and I nodded to her. She gave me a warm greeting.

"So good to see you," she said. "It was weird being here without you. We shot some scenes, but there aren't too many without you in them."

I chuckled. "I don't know if that's good or not."

We were all laughing when the scene started, and they had to get the camera guys to wait while we composed ourselves. I felt in a good mood today and it seemed the others did, too – whether they caught it from me or not, I couldn't tell.

At lunchtime, Bennet was excited. He said he'd had a call for me from Gerard – I'd put him through to the other number while I was working, since I couldn't just stop mid-scene and answer my telephone – and I couldn't wait to hear what it was.

"He says he's going to do the photo-session in Oldham."

"What?" I stared. I couldn't believe it. That would be amazing! It would save us having to try and sneak off somewhere for two days. It would be absolutely perfect, and it would fit, too.

We weren't city people, and I'd been portraying myself like that for too long. I thought that the public personality I had lived for so many years was another act – a part I was playing constantly; that people had expected me to play for my whole existence. Now, finally, I got to show myself for who I really am. And I couldn't wait for it to begin.

Bennet and I discussed a bit longer and I took the chance to call Gerard and confirm a time with him. He agreed to next week. He'd be able to fly out to Colorado Springs.

We finished lunch and I took the opportunity to talk to the director as soon as I got to the set. We were shooting in the house again, and he was standing by the door, a sheet of paper in hand, chatting with the guys in charge of acoustics. I waited for him to finish before asking him.

"Next week?" he said. He sounded mad, but he wasn't mad after I'd explained it would only be a few hours, and that it would be here, and I wouldn't have to go anywhere.

When I'd finished telling him about it, he gave me a firm look.

"Okay," he said. "But if you're gone for longer than two hours, I'll want to know why. And please don't do any photos on set," he added. "I don't want anyone seeing the sets before we get the trailers out."

"Sure," I said. I hadn't even thought about where we might shoot yet, but it wouldn't have occurred to me to do it in any of the houses we were using for the film settings.

I was relieved that he didn't mind and that everything was getting so well organized.

The photographers arrived the next week. Gerard met us in the town, his big glasses making his eyes seem immensely large for his face, as usual. I grinned to see him. He was older than me, and he had a formidable reputation in the press world. I was very lucky to have him as my agent.

"Okay," he said. He looked at Bennet, who was standing next to me, seeming scared. He smiled. "Hell. He's really got something. And I think we can really work with this, now that I see the guy."

Bennet went pink and I smiled at him. "Yeah, he is good looking."

Bennet was still blushing as we went to stand in front of an old building. Gerard had discussed with us and we'd decided to choose places that could be anywhere; not particularly referencing Old West architecture, but with a neutral feel to them. I felt my heart glow with love as I stood next to Stuart at the wall of one of the old buildings.

The session lasted for just on two hours, after which time we were all exhausted, Gerard and the cameraman at least as exhausted as we were.

"That was hectic," I said to Bennet as we led Gerard back to the car-park. The camera-guys were walking behind, carrying the heavy bags with their cameras and lenses in them. Bennet grinned.

"Absolutely it was," he agreed. "It was strange."

I chuckled. "It must have been," I said. I looked at him, thinking that he had actually enjoyed it. His face was bright, eyes shining. I hadn't seen him look that excited about something for a long while.

"Weirdly, I enjoyed it, too," he said.

I smiled. "I'm not surprised. Everyone thought you did so well. You're a natural." I saw him grin and I nodded. "You really are. I am used to photos but you responded so brilliantly. You really should consider acting professionally."

"No," he said with a laugh, but I thought he was considering it, and I thought that was a good thing.

We went back to the filming, but luckily there was only one more scene with me in it to shoot for the day, and it only took an hour to get it done. I went straight to the restaurant, where we had agreed Bennet and I would meet for a drink as soon as filming was done.

"I'm glad we did that," he said as he poured a beer for himself. I nodded.

"Me, too," I said. It was five o' clock, I was tired but I was also happy. I lifted my glass and tapped it to his own.

He grinned. "It's so good to be here with you," he said softly.

"And for me to be here with you," I said. I looked at him, here in the familiar space of our favorite restaurant. I felt my heart flood with feelings that were so intense I could barely contain them, and yet were also gentle and warm and the nicest things that I had ever felt. I looked into his eyes, and I didn't notice the surroundings anymore, or hear the waiter recommending dishes at the next table, or notice the smell of delicious food wafting from the kitchen. All I could think of, all I knew about, was the man sitting across the table from me.

"Stuart," he said gently.

"I love you," I said.

He looked at me and I looked at him and I could see surprise in his eyes, as well as delight, and joy, and so many expressions that were almost too complicated to read, but all of them glad.

"I love you," he said.

He leaned forward and I leaned against him, resting my forehead on his own, feeling a love so profound that I didn't have words for it flooding through my body. I sat there and I knew with absolute certainty that I had never expected in my life to feel so wonderful. It was amazing to discover what was possible when one opened one's heart. I had learned to love, and to trust, and in so doing had found my true self and the man I loved the most and that was the greatest thing I could ever have thought possible.

Chapter 15: Bennet

I woke up beside Stuart. He was asleep, which was unusual – normally, he woke up first and sneaked out of bed and went to the shower. But this morning, I woke first and carefully slid up the bed to sitting. His eyelids fluttered.

"You're awake," I murmured.

He laughed. "You still can't sneak out before me."

I chuckled and lay down beside him. "And you haven't managed to sneak out before me, too. So there."

We both laughed. I snuggled up next to him and we lay there until he stretched, then kissed me and slid back on the pillows.

"We should shower," he said.

I grinned. "If you have finally found a shower-gel you actually like." I was still laughing about how fussy he was – we had gone through two in the last week because he couldn't stand the smell of them. I'd ended up having to give them to other people. He had finally settled on a nice-scented one with a fancy mahogany-colored bottle. I hoped he would stick with it for a while.

"Yeah," he said. "I like this one. Let's go."

We went to the shower and I felt my skin tingle as he watched me undress. I was only wearing boxers, but my face still reddened as he watched me.

We showered and dressed. It would have been nice to slip into bed for another hour or two, but we both seemed a little restless and we went down to the kitchen together. I blinked at the bright sunshine flowing in through the windows – it was a beautiful Colorado summertime, and the sunshine was nice, even at this time of the morning.

"Coffee?" he asked as I sat down at the kitchen table. I chuckled.

"Yes, please."

We had a proper coffee-pot now; neither of us even thinking of anything even vaguely less-organic than fresh-ground coffee. We had gone for simple things since moving to Colorado – it had been amazing to find this house. We'd both loved it instantly, and, if the fittings were old, we could replace them. It was an absolute bargain – or so Stuart said, though my eyes had widened at the price. He had said it was a nice price for a house like this, and I believed him.

Sitting in the kitchen now, I thought the same thing. I don't think anybody could have argued with the fact that we had an absolutely stunning view. It was beautiful. I could see the distant hills and the wide expanse of pebbly ground and the one or two trees that stood out of the magnificent surroundings. I looked across at Stuart and grinned.

"It's beautiful here," I sighed.

He nodded. "It is," he said. "But it isn't what recommends the place to me." His eyes were shining as they looked at me and I felt warmth fill my heart. I had known him for two years now, and each day I looked at that stunning man I found more to love about him. Maybe some people would have found it annoying that he snored, for example, but I loved it – somehow it made him seem more real and therefore more loveable.

"Me too," I said.

He stood to get the coffee and we both sat and drank. The taste was rich and bitter and I shut my eyes, enjoying it.

Stuart leaned back in the chair, looking up at the beams. We had a beautiful ceiling with proper beams throughout the house. I really liked being able to see them. Everything about the place felt natural and strong, so different to the somehow-artificial houses I'd grown up in.

"Do you have to work today?" he asked me.

I shook my head. I had started as a commentator for theater and movies – it was something my degree suited me perfectly to do, and something that I'd found I really liked. My reviews turned out well and were being published in two magazines already. I could barely believe how my life had transformed.

"Good," he said. "Then we can do something."

"Yeah!" I agreed. I thought that it would be good to take a walk or something – we both really loved hiking, and it was one of the things that we took the opportunity to do when we were both not working.

"Great," Stuart said, tipping his head back to drain the coffee from the coffee-cup. He stood to start making breakfast. We took it in turns, though I had to admit that my attempts were not nearly as elaborate as his – I was happy just to have muesli or toast.

"So," I asked as we sat eating breakfast together. "How is work on your side?"

He grinned. "I'm so looking forward to that new job."

I smiled too. He had recently been offered a role in a new movie – it was a quieter, gentler role and I thought it suited him perfectly. It was still set in the same sort of cowboy-town setting, but it wasn't like his usual shoot-ups-and-bar-fight sort of movie. It was a deeper, more feeling role and I thought the part was much more like himself. The real Stuart Glendon.

"I'm excited to see it."

"I'm glad you won't comment on it," he said. Ever since I started the job as a reviewer, we had agreed not to comment on his work. I wasn't going to be able to be unbiased about it, and I thought it was better if I didn't review it.

I smiled. "You know what I think already," I said.

He grinned. "I know you'd be too nice as a reviewer of my work."

I tilted my head sideways. "I don't think it would be possible to be too nice about your work, dearest."

He laughed and leaned forward and kissed me. "Well, sweetie, I think I might be inclined not to agree."

We both chuckled and he stood and I stood too and we went to the window, looking out. I could feel his arm around me and I thought that I had never imagined being as fulfilled as this. I had never thought

I would find someone I loved as much as this. I would never have dreamed that so much was possible if you trust what your heart knows.

*****

Enjoy what you read? Please keep flipping to the end of the book to leave a review. Thanks!

Don't miss out!

Visit the website below and you can sign up to receive emails whenever Van Cole publishes a new book. There's no charge and no obligation.

https://books2read.com/r/B-A-RTRV-YVSJC

Connecting independent readers to independent writers.

Also by Van Cole

3 Man Huddle: MMM Best Friend Romance
His Alpha Wolf: Gay First Time Romance
A Dragon's Miracle: Gay Dragon MPREG Romance
Double-Teamed: MMM First Time Football Romance
His Football Star: Gay Second Chance Romance
Love In My Town: MM First Time Romance
Training A Hockey Star
Game Night
Double Shift
Take A Shot
Dear Professor
Getting Inked
Ninth Inning
Triple Threat
Seducing My Best Friend's Brother
My Protector
The Blueprint
Show Me The Way
End Zone
Matched To His Tiger
Love At First Puck
My Straight Boss
Falling For The Alpha
My Boss

www.ingramcontent.com/pod-product-compliance
Lightning Source LLC
Chambersburg PA
CBHW022013150726

47990CB00002B/632